"We should get ba
down from the hil... ...ng
for his help.

"I don't usually come on so strong," Logan said, fumbling for something to ease the awkwardness.

"Don't apologize. It was fine."

No woman had ever described his kiss as fine.

Sadie stopped when they reached the back porch. "Okay, here's the truth." She looked him in the eye. "I liked your kiss. More than is probably smart, but..." She stared at her feet. "I don't want an affair or a fling or a rendezvous or whatever else it's called these days."

"What do you want?"

"I want forever with a man I can depend on. A man who will come through for me and the boys. Who'll make us a priority not an afterthought." She nodded to the back door. "It's time for me and the boys to go."

"Back to Wisconsin?"

"No, to my aunt's house." Sadie disappeared inside, leaving Logan standing outside feeling like an idiot.

Dear Reader,

I can't imagine what it's like to be the mother of twins—I had my hands full raising a son and daughter who were born nineteen months apart. Mothers of identical twins face different challenges when raising their children and the one that fascinates me most is nurturing each child's individuality. In *Twins for the Texas Rancher* Sadie feels as if she's failing as a parent because she spends much of her energy and time trying to manage Tommy's ADD, while Tyler is often overlooked.

Mothers are superhuman—I really believe this. But the downside of our ability to raise children, manage a household and hold down a job is that we become so good at it that we're reluctant to ask for help, because we see it as a weakness or we're afraid doing anything different will upset the status quo. It's only when Sadie loses her job and lands in Stampede, Texas, that she learns it takes a family to raise a child and that sometimes it's the messes we create in life that lead us down a path we might never have taken otherwise. In Sadie's case, Logan's messes are what lead them to their very own happy-ever-after.

If you missed the first book in the Cowboys of Stampede, Texas series, *The Cowboy's Accidental Baby* (May 2017), you can find out more about that story and other books I've written at marinthomas.com.

Happy reading,

Marin Thomas

TWINS FOR THE TEXAS RANCHER

Marin Thomas

Recycling programs
for this product may
not exist in your area.

ISBN-13: 978-0-373-75775-6

Twins for the Texas Rancher

Copyright © 2017 by Brenda Smith-Beagley

Printed in U.S.A.

www.Harlequin.com

Marin Thomas grew up in the Midwest, then attended college at the U of A in Tucson, Arizona, where she earned a BA in radio-TV and played basketball for the Lady Wildcats. Following graduation, she married her college sweetheart in the historic Little Chapel of the West in Las Vegas, Nevada. Recent empty-nesters, Marin and her husband now live in Texas, where cattle is king, cowboys are plentiful and pickups rule the road. Visit her on the web at marinthomas.com.

Books by Marin Thomas

Harlequin Western Romance

The Cowboys of Stampede, Texas

The Cowboy's Accidental Baby

Harlequin American Romance

Cowboys of the Rio Grande

A Cowboy's Redemption
The Surgeon's Christmas Baby
A Cowboy's Claim

The Cash Brothers

The Cowboy Next Door
Twins Under the Christmas Tree
Her Secret Cowboy
The Cowboy's Destiny
True Blue Cowboy
A Cowboy of Her Own

Visit the Author Profile page
at Harlequin.com for more titles.

To all the mothers who've given birth to
multiples—you ladies are rock stars!

Chapter One

"Are we lost, Mom?"

"Nope," Sadie McHenry fibbed. She glanced in the rearview mirror at her son Tyler. The clip light attached to his book, *Frog and Toad Are Friends*, illuminated his worried little face.

"We're taking the long way," she said. It was almost midnight, and according to the GPS on her iPhone they should have arrived in Stampede, Texas, a half hour ago. When she'd passed the sign for Rocky Point, she realized she'd taken a wrong turn somewhere. "Is Tommy sleeping?"

"Uh-huh."

Her four-year-old blue-eyed, brown-haired twins might be the spitting image of each other, but every day of their lives was another chapter in the tortoise and the hare story. Tyler was sober, quiet and shy. Tommy was outgoing, strangers were his best friends, and walls were made to bounce off.

Last year when she'd enrolled them in preschool, Tyler had come home the first day with a good-student award, while Tommy had broken the record for the number of minutes spent in the time-out chair—twelve. The teacher had recommended Tommy be tested for attention deficit disorder, and sure enough, at three years of age her son had shown signs of ADD. After several months of applying disciplinary techniques suggested by Tommy's pediatrician, there had been little change in his behavior and the teacher had grown frustrated, so Sadie had withdrawn the boys and enrolled them in a different preschool program.

"Are you tired?"

"I'm fine, honey." Tyler was a sweet boy and it broke her heart that she couldn't focus more attention on him because she was constantly monitoring and containing Tommy's wild ways. "Close your eyes and rest. Tomorrow we'll see Aunt Lydia and Great-Aunt Amelia." Aunt Lydia was actually a cousin, but the boys had become confused when she'd explained how they were all related, so aside from their grandparents everyone was an aunt or an uncle.

Not a mile had passed since leaving Madison, Wisconsin, that Sadie hadn't second-guessed her decision to drive to Stampede. She'd called ahead and warned her aunt and cousin Lydia of her impending visit. If anyone understood Sadie's need to jump off the crazy train and catch her breath, it was her other cousin Scarlett. She had a front-row seat to Sadie's frenzied life—parenting twins with little help from her ex, working forty hours a week, then spending Saturday and Sunday catching up on the laundry and shopping. Throw in an emergency doctor visit, a missed child-support payment or a flat tire and the crazy train derailed.

A sliver of guilt pricked her. She hadn't yet told her parents that she'd been laid off because she knew they'd insist she and the twins move to Florida, where they could better meddle in her life. She'd planned to look for another job, but then the director of the boys' new preschool had suggested she register Tommy in a special program for kids with ADD, insisting he'd benefit from the extra attention. The recommendation made sense except without a job Sadie couldn't afford the higher tuition and because it was already the end of August, enrollment for the program was closed. Tommy had been placed on a waiting list for the spring semester. With the lease on her apartment up for renewal and Tommy having difficulties in school, Sadie had packed up their belongings and put them into storage so she and her boys could take a much needed break from life.

Tommy's troubles made her feel like a failure as a mother. She worried that if she didn't get a handle on Tommy's behavior by the time he entered full-day kindergarten in just over a year, he'd risk being held back. Splitting up the boys would only create a new set of problems for her to deal with.

The rain finally let up, and Sadie loosened her death grip on the wheel, then switched the wipers off. If not for having to drive through several downpours after leaving San Antonio, they would have made better time.

"Mom?"

"Yes, Tyler?"

"Is Dad gonna miss us?"

"Of course he will, honey."

She took several slow, deep breaths, a trick she'd used to help keep her calm when Tommy tried her patience. The day the boys had been born, Sadie's stress level skyrocketed and had remained high ever since. As if giving birth to twins wasn't enough strain on a working mother, being married to a man who had never pitched in had made her days even more taxing. But that hadn't even been the worst part—Pete had been disloyal. The first time she learned he'd cheated on her, she'd been eight months pregnant. For her sons' sake, and because being a single mother of twins had terrified her, she'd given Pete a second chance. Two years later he'd "slipped up" again—his words, not hers. Marriage wasn't a game of baseball, so after two strikes she called him out.

"If you want to talk to your father while we're visiting Aunt Amelia, let me know and I'll call him."

Silence greeted her offer.

She had no regrets about the divorce. Pete had spent so little time with the boys that they'd barely noticed a difference when he'd moved out of the apartment. And they didn't think it odd that they saw him only the second Wednesday and third weekend of each month—that was, when Pete didn't cancel on them. Not only did her ex go back on his promises to his sons, but he was often late paying his share of the preschool bill. When that happened, she had to cover his portion, then wait a week or more until he paid her back.

If there was anything good about the boys growing accustomed to their father's absence in their everyday lives, it was that they hadn't objected when Pete had announced his plans to move to Baltimore with his girlfriend. Sadie admitted that it was difficult to watch her ex date—not because she was jealous of the other women, but because she was envious of Pete never having to worry that the twins might sabotage his relationship. Sadie's two brief forays into dating had ended immediately after she informed the men she was a mother of twins.

Learning that her cousin Lydia had married the infamous Gunner Hardell, Stampede's notorious bad boy—a man who'd flirted with rodeo and hadn't planned on settling down and having children—gave Sadie hope that one day she'd meet a guy who was willing to be a father to her boys. She wouldn't care what he looked like or what he did for a living as long as he was dependable and helped make her life easier, not more stressful.

"Who's Amelia?"

No surprise that Tyler didn't ask any more questions about his father.

"She's your great-grandmother's sister. You can call her Aunt Amelia." The boys had just turned two when she'd taken them to Texas for the first time. Back then, she'd needed to regroup after she'd filed for divorce, and she'd chosen to visit her aunt instead of her parents, who'd moved to an adult community in Fort Lauderdale, Florida.

She wished she was closer to her mother and father, but she'd disappointed them badly when she'd become pregnant Neither of them liked Pete and they'd offered to help Sadie financially if she didn't marry the babies' father. But Sadie hadn't wanted to be a single mom, and Pete had been willing to give marriage a try, so they'd tied the knot, hoping for the best. Unlike her parents, Aunt Amelia had always treated Sadie warmly and hadn't judged her for the mistakes she'd made. It was only natural that her great-aunt was the first person Sadie would turn to when her life was crumbling around her.

"You'll like Aunt Amelia's house. She has a lovely attic that I played in with your aunt Scarlett and aunt Lydia when we were kids." Every summer, Sadie had tagged along when her grandmother visited her eldest sister in Stampede for a month. She had fond memories of running around in the big Victorian.

"What's an attic?"

"A secret room tucked up under the roof."

"Are Poppa and Nana gonna be there?"

"Nope. They're leaving tomorrow on an Alaskan cruise." Sadie's parents had visited Madison for a week in May, carving out two afternoons to spend with the boys. Because they'd insisted Tommy was too difficult to handle, Sadie had used two of her vacation days to join their visit to the zoo and a museum, where she'd been subjected to her mother's parenting lectures. She'd been told that if she didn't get a handle on Tommy's behavior, he'd end up serving time in a juvenile detention center. Poor Tyler hadn't been mentioned at all, as if he didn't even exist. Needless to say she'd been relieved when her folks left town, and she wouldn't have to see them until Christmas.

"What did you do in the attic?" Tyler asked.

"We played school and pretended we were trapped in a castle waiting for Prince Charming to rescue us." She peeked in the mirror and Tyler's big blue eyes blinked at her. He was a worrier just like her.

"Can I read in an attic?"

"Of course you can." Tyler had learned to read before Tommy and at first Sadie had believed it was because he was smarter. Then one evening Tyler had been reading on the living-room floor, and Tommy had thrown a Lego block at his head to get his attention.

Tyler hadn't even flinched. It was then that she understood her son's obsession with books. The only time Tyler was able to escape the chaos that followed his brother everywhere was when he was lost in a story. With such different personalities she often wondered how long it would be before the boys drifted apart.

Sadie's thoughts shifted back to work and her stomach churned. Surely it wouldn't be difficult to find another job when she returned to Madison. She'd worked in Dr. Kennedy's dental office the past five years as a bookkeeper/office manager and had been caught by surprise when he'd announced he was merging his practice with another dentist and her job was being eliminated. Dr. Kennedy had offered her a generous severance package, which included six months' income and health insurance coverage for her and the boys, so she had time to find another job and a place for them to live.

"Is Dad gonna come to Aunt Amelia's house?" Her little copilot refused to go to sleep.

"I don't think so. Baltimore is a long way from Texas." The boys and their father had said their goodbyes last month when Pete had stopped at the apartment with toys from the dollar store. The schmuck had enough money to wine and dine his new ladylove, but he couldn't buy a decent parting gift for his sons. If he'd paid more attention to the twins, he'd know that one of them preferred books over plastic toy boats.

Sadie had asked Pete not to tell the boys he was moving in with his girlfriend and her three children— she'd wanted to break the news to them in her own time. But he'd ignored her request and had brought along one of the woman's sons that afternoon, which had opened the door to a million questions about why Dad was living with another little boy and not them. Pete promised the twins they could visit him at Thanksgiving, but when Sadie had asked if he planned to pay for the plane tickets, he'd balked and amended his promise to *hopefully* seeing the boys during the holidays.

"We'll find lots of things to do to in Stampede to keep busy," she said. But not too busy. Sadie was looking forward to sitting still, sipping her aunt's lemonade and catching up with her cousin Lydia, who was expecting her first child next spring.

When the exit for Stampede came up, Sadie lifted her foot from the gas and veered off the highway and onto a frontage road that led to the Moonlight Motel. She drove another three miles before a blue neon moon came into view in the distance. "Vacancy" flashed in the middle of the sign and she breathed a sigh of relief.

If she hadn't gotten lost, run into bad weather and had to make an emergency stop along the highway so Tommy could pee, they'd have arrived before dark. But because Tommy hadn't pulled his pants down far enough he'd soaked his jeans and by the time she'd located a clean pair of pants in their luggage and gotten back on the road, they'd lost an hour of daylight.

She stopped in front of the motel office and shifted the van into Park, then turned off the engine. Four vehicles sat in front of the six rooms. Hopefully that meant two rooms were still available.

"Are we here?" Tyler asked.

"Yep. This is the motel that Aunt Lydia just renovated." She unsnapped her seat belt. "We're sleeping here tonight, because both of your aunts are already in bed and I don't want to wake them." She opened her door. "Stay in the car with your brother while I see if they have a room for us."

Sadie made sure she locked the van, then entered the office. When she stepped inside, the handle slipped from her grasp and the door banged closed. The sound woke the dark-haired man who'd been asleep in a rocking chair. He bolted upright, brown eyes blinking.

Lydia had texted photos of her and Gunner after they'd gotten married in Las Vegas a few weeks ago, and this man wasn't him although he looked around her age. "I'm sorry I startled you." She flashed an apologetic smile.

He rubbed a hand over his chiseled face, wiping his sleepy expression away. Then he stared at his sock feet for a moment before sitting back down in the rocker again and shoving his feet into a pair of worn cowboy boots.

"Apologies for falling asleep on the job." He unfolded his frame and stood. He was tall, a little over six feet, and the breadth of his shoulders suggested that monitoring a motel wasn't his true occupation. His long strides ate up the distance between the rocker and the check-in desk. Her gaze latched on to the shirttail sticking out of the waistband of his Wranglers, which fit him very nicely.

"The sign said vacancy, so I'm hoping you have a room available with two double beds."

"All the rooms have double beds." He rubbed the five-o'clock shadow covering his cheeks. "I'm filling in for my brother tonight, but I'm sure I can figure out how to register you."

"You don't look anything like Gunner."

His head jerked up. "You know my brother?"

"We haven't officially met, but he's married to my cousin. You must be either Logan or Reid."

"Logan."

"Sadie McHenry." She stepped up to the desk and offered her hand. "I think the last time I saw you and your brothers was at my great-uncle's funeral years ago."

"That seems about right." He kept hold of her hand while his warm gaze traveled over her.

"I visited my aunt two years ago, but we didn't run into each other that time." When she wiggled her fingers, his grip tightened, and the warm friction from the calluses on his palm sent a flutter up her arm. She swallowed a wistful sigh when the tingles fanned through her chest. Embarrassed by her reaction, she tugged her hand free and pressed her fingers against her thigh.

"Is Lydia expecting you tonight?" Logan bent down and searched for something beneath the counter.

"No. I told her and Aunt Amelia not to expect us until tomorrow, but I decided to drive straight through."

Logan set a notepad with the motel logo on it next to the keyboard and then picked up a pen. He must have changed his mind about whatever he'd intended to write down because he put the pen back into a drawer and moved the notepad to the other side of the desk.

"Lydia did a great job fixing up the place." Sadie looked around the office.

"She impressed my grandfather, which isn't easy to do." Logan took the pen out of the drawer again and set it on the counter. "Don't listen to Gunner when he tells you that he did most of the work. Lydia hired a professional to do the heavy lifting. My brother just got in the way."

"I heard my cousin and Gunner are splitting their time between the motel and the downtown apartment they're renovating."

Logan nodded. "They're here tonight. I can wake them up if you —"

"No, that's okay. I'll see them in the morning."

Logan came out from behind the desk and walked across the room. "Lydia found these old post office boxes at a flea market and had Gunner spray-paint them." He opened one. "They're using them to store tourist brochures." He gathered a handful of pamphlets and passed them to Sadie. "In case you get bored while you're in town." He smiled, offering Sadie a glimpse of straight white teeth.

"Thanks." She glanced outside at the van. "About getting a room for the night…"

"Sorry." Logan returned to the counter and pecked at the keyboard. "Stupid computer."

"I parked close to room 1 if that's available."

"Room 1 is Lydia and Gunner's personal room." Maybe it was the soft glow of the pendant light hanging over the desk, but Sadie swore a red tinge spread across Logan's cheeks. "Gunner made the room into a combination office-nursery as a surprise for Lydia. He intends to take the baby to work with him when Lydia has appointments with her design clients."

Gunner plans on helping out with the baby? Sadie could count on one hand the number of times Pete had fed, changed, bathed or burped the twins. She hadn't minded caring for two babies while on maternity leave, but a little help from the father after returning to her day job would have been appreciated.

Logan punched several numbers into a device before swiping a key card and then handing it to her. "You're in room 6."

She put the card into the back pocket of her jeans. "How much for one night?"

"A hundred and ten, but family stays for free." Logan winked and Sadie started.

"Umm…" She couldn't remember the last time a man had winked at her. What did that even mean these days?

"I'll help you with your luggage." He walked over to the door.

Sadie was used to doing all the heavy lifting since her divorce, but tonight she was tired enough to accept a helping hand. "Thank you."

He followed her to the van and as soon as the door slid open, Tommy pushed Tyler aside and jumped to the ground. Lucky her, the boys had learned how to get out of their booster seats a year ago. "Who are you?" Tommy asked.

"This is your cousin, but you can call him Uncle Logan." She helped Tyler to the ground. "My sons, Tommy—" she pointed to the steel trash container by the office door that Tommy was attempting to climb "—and Tyler." He stood by her, his hand clutching her thigh.

Logan's gaze zigzagged between the twins. "You guys look alike."

"That's 'cause we're twins," Tommy said.

Keeping a straight face as he stared at Tyler, Logan teased, "What's a twin?"

Tyler opened his mouth to answer, but Tommy beat him to the punch. "Us." He pointed to Tyler, then poked a finger in his own chest. "We're twins 'cause we came out of my mom's stomach at the same time."

Now that Logan had that nice image in his head, Sadie said, "Grab your backpacks, boys."

Tommy raced past Logan and dived into the van, then tossed out Tyler's backpack—the one with an image of a Labrador retriever wearing reading glasses on the front. The second one to hit the ground sported an image of Captain America.

Sadie removed a small overnight bag and Logan took it from her. "Is this it?" he asked.

"The rest of the luggage can stay in the van." She slung her purse over her shoulder, then pressed the automatic lock button on the key fob. "Should I park the van in front of our room?"

"It'll be fine right here." Logan frowned. "It's just the three of you?"

"Yes." It had always felt like it had been only her and the boys, even before she'd divorced Pete. "Why?"

He glanced at the license plate on the van. "That was a long drive to make by yourselves."

Tommy patted Logan's thigh. "My dad moved to Balkimore."

"Baltimore." Sadie looked at Logan. "Didn't Lydia mention that I was divorced?"

"I'm sure she did, and I forgot," he said. "Your room is at the end." Logan pointed to the door and Tommy raced down the sidewalk. Sadie took Tyler's hand and they followed behind Logan. When Tommy stopped at the wrong door, Logan said, "One more, buddy."

Instead of numbers on the rooms there were placards. "Stagecoach?" Sadie asked.

Logan held his hand out for the key card and Sadie gave it to him. "Lydia named each of the rooms after a Western movie."

"Clever idea," she said.

He slid the card into the lock reader, then opened the door and flipped on the light before standing back and allowing her and the boys to enter first.

"Wow." Sadie admired the Western mural of John Wayne sitting on horseback in the desert. "Amazing." She ran her fingers lightly over the image. "That's wallpaper."

The sound of the toilet flushing echoed in the room, then Tommy walked into view, pulling up his pants. "The toilet works, Mom."

"Stop." Sadie pointed to the sink outside the bathroom. Tommy turned around and washed his hands, then shook them dry before dashing across the room and launching himself onto the bed.

"Shoes," Sadie said. Tommy kicked off his sneakers and began jumping on the mattress.

"C'mon, Tyler. Don't you want to jump with me?"

Tyler inched closer to Sadie, his eyes still watching Logan.

"Settle down." She braced herself for the inevitable dark scowl that Tommy's behavior usually garnered from strangers. Instead Logan's mouth broke into a wide grin as he watched her son use the bed for a trampoline.

"You're encouraging him," Sadie whispered.

Logan looked her way, his gaze slipping to her bosom before returning to her face. "What?"

"Stop smiling."

He pressed his lips together and narrowed his eyes. "Better?"

"Much."

"Tomorrow you should let the kids check out the playground behind the motel."

"That's a good idea." Sadie nudged Tyler toward the bathroom. "Your turn." He obeyed, like he always did, closing the door behind him.

"Is there anything else I can get you? More towels? An extra blanket?" Logan asked.

"I think we'll be fine for one night." She expected him to leave—actually, she was surprised he hadn't bolted for the door as soon as Tommy dived onto the bed. Instead he appeared reluctant to go.

Tommy did a backflip and Logan clapped. "You'd make a good circus clown." He waited until Tyler finished washing his hands, then said, "And you'd be a good circus manager."

Tommy rolled off the bed. "What's a circus manager?"

"Enough questions for one day, kiddo," Sadie said. "Get your pj's on and crawl under the covers." For once, Tommy listened to her and followed Tyler's lead, digging his clothes out of his backpack.

"It's pretty safe around here, but make sure you use the bolt and bar latch before you turn out the lights."

"I'll do that right now." Sadie smiled. "It was nice seeing you, again."

"Hey, Uncle Logan." Tommy ran across the room,

his pajama bottoms on backward. He pointed at Logan's boots. "Are you a real cowboy?"

"I am."

"Do you got a horse?"

"I do."

"Does he got a name?"

"*Her* name is Sweet Pea."

"You got a girl horse?"

"Yep."

"That sucks."

"We talked about using that word, young man." Tommy had learned it from one of the kids at school.

"I wanna boy horse." He looked at Sadie. "I want to see Sweet Pea."

Logan answered before Sadie had a chance to. "You and Tyler are welcome to visit her at the ranch."

"Stop pestering Uncle Logan. It's way past bedtime."

Logan opened the door, then glanced around Sadie. "Hey, Tyler, have you ever been in a hayloft?"

Tyler shook his head, clutching the Frog and Toad book against his chest.

"If you come out to the ranch, bring your books because it's a cool place to read."

Sadie appreciated how Logan made a point to speak to Tyler. More often than not, Tommy stole the show and his brother was forgotten.

"I'm sure we'll be making a trip to the ranch to see the horses and the hayloft," Sadie said.

Logan shut the door and then Sadie secured the extra locks. "Time to play the quiet game and see who falls asleep first. The winner gets an extra doughnut for breakfast tomorrow." She didn't like using bribes, but it beat yelling all the time. The boys snuggled beneath the blankets and closed their eyes, pretending to sleep.

She kissed their foreheads. "I love you, guys."

*Me, too*s echoed in her ear.

Sadie carried her nightshirt and a clean pair of panties into the bathroom and took a shower. Afterward, she adjusted the air conditioner so the room wouldn't grow too cold during the night. She left the bathroom door halfway open and kept the light on in case the boys got up in the middle of the night to use the toilet.

"Mom?" Tommy whispered.

"You're supposed to be sleeping."

"Can we go see Uncle Logan's girl horse tomorrow?"

"I don't know, honey."

"Mom?"

"What?" A full minute passed and only the quiet hum of the air conditioner filled the room. "Tommy?" she whispered. No answer.

Her little Energizer Bunny had finally drifted off to sleep.

Now if only she could get some rest. But when Sadie closed her eyes, she saw Logan's face. In her meager dating experience, single handsome men weren't jumping at the chance to interact with a challenging child as rambunctious as Tommy.

Don't forget Tyler.

Sadie was amazed that Logan had picked up on Tyler's love of reading after just meeting him. As she drifted off to sleep, she couldn't help thinking how great it would be to find a man who wanted to be a father to her boys and would treat them better than the one they already had.

Chapter Two

Logan glanced at the clock on the wall and rubbed his eyes. Five a.m. He pushed himself out of the rocking chair and stretched until the twinges and aches disappeared. He was only thirty-two and suspected he'd be in worse shape if he'd continued rodeoing all these years. *At least the aches and pains would have been worth it.* After his father had been struck and killed by a hit-and-run driver while changing a flat tire on the side of the road and his grandfather fell off the wagon, Logan had stashed away his rodeo gear and returned home to ride fence and feed cattle.

If Gunner didn't waltz into the office by six, he'd lock the doors and take off. His brother had been keeping honeymoon hours since he and Lydia returned from Vegas. *Married.* Logan shook his head in disbelief that his baby brother—the family goof-off, the guy who'd boasted he'd never let a woman catch him—hadn't only gotten married, but he was going to be a father.

Speaking of kids… Logan's thoughts switched to the Stagecoach room and Sadie. The top of the blue-eyed blonde's head barely reached his shoulder, but one glance at her curvy hips and full bosom and there was no mistaking she was a full-grown woman.

And a mother of twins.

The boys were a handful. Tommy reminded Logan of himself as a kid—always on the go. Tyler was more like the middle Hardell brother, Reid—quiet and watchful. No one ever knew what Reid was thinking, but he was always aware of what was going on around him.

Logan prepared a fresh pot of coffee in case any of the guests wanted a cup before hitting the road, and then he went into the small bathroom in the hallway and opened his dopp kit. After he erased his five-o'clock shadow with his electric shaver, he brushed his teeth and gargled with mouthwash. Back in the office, he stared out the window. The sun was beginning to rise and it looked like someone had taken a giant brush and painted a swath of pink across the horizon.

C'mon, Gunner. Get out of bed.

Out of the corner of his eye he saw something race past the rooms outside. He opened the lobby door just in time to see the backside of a little person tearing around the corner of the motel.

Tommy.

What was the kid doing up this early in the morning? Logan left the office, glancing down the sidewalk to the Stagecoach room. From across the parking lot it looked as if the kid had left the door cracked open. Logan doubted Sadie even knew her son had escaped. When he walked behind the motel he found Tommy, his pajama bottoms still on backward, standing on the playground swing.

As soon as the boy realized he wasn't alone, he shouted, "Uncle Logan, push me!"

Uncle Logan. The moniker squeezed his heart and not in a good way. Logan walked behind the swing. "Sit down and I'll give you an underduck."

The boy dropped to the seat. "What's an under-duck?"

"Hold on tight, and I'll show you." Logan pulled the swing back, then ran forward, pushing the seat up and over his head. Tommy squealed. "Do it again, Uncle Logan!"

He ignored the command and said, "You're awake awful early this morning."

No answer.

"Is your mother up?"

"I don't know."

He had a feeling Tommy's standard response to most questions was *I don't know.* "Are you hungry?"

"Mom said we could have doughnuts for breakfast 'cause we went to sleep fast."

Logan expected Sadie to appear any moment, searching for her son. But five minutes had passed and she hadn't made an appearance.

"I wanna stop, Uncle Logan."

He stepped forward and caught the swing. "C'mon, I'll walk you to the room."

"I don't want to go back to sleep."

Logan hadn't only noticed how pretty Sadie was last night when she'd checked her and the boys into the motel. He'd also noted the dark circles beneath her eyes. The drive from Wisconsin to Texas had exhausted her. "Tell you what," he said. "You and I will go get the doughnuts." *And let your mother and brother catch up on sleep.*

Logan took Tommy's hand and returned to the office, where he wrote two sticky notes explaining that he and Tommy had gone down the road to the Valero to buy everyone breakfast. He stuck one note on Gunner and Lydia's door and the other one, which had his cell phone number on it, against the inside of Sadie's door before he quietly closed it all the way.

"What about my booster seat?" Tommy asked when Logan opened the door of his pickup. His gaze swung to the white minivan. The safety seats were locked inside.

"I think I have something that might work. Follow me." He and Tommy went behind the desk and down the hallway to the storage closet. "I bought this for my brother and your aunt's baby." Logan pulled the tarp off a box. "This is the Cadillac of all car seats, kid." Logan had spent a small fortune on the contraption that claimed to be a five-point-harness seat and later converted into a booster seat once a kid reached forty pounds. "How much do you weigh?" he asked.

Tommy shrugged, then pointed to the image on the box. "That's a baby. I'm not a baby."

"I think this will work for a short trip." He opened the box and removed the seat, then detached the top portion meant for younger kids and infants. "Let's see if I can figure out how to install the booster seat."

It took several tries and a few swallowed cusswords before Logan had the contraption secured in the back seat and Tommy strapped in.

"You look like a trussed-up turkey."

"I look like a baby." The boy's mouth turned down in a pout.

Logan ignored him and climbed behind the wheel. The Valero was ten miles down the road and Tommy talked the entire fifteen-minute drive. By the time he parked in front of the convenience mart, Logan's ears were hurting. It wasn't until they entered the store that he saw his sidekick was barefoot. "What happened to your shoes?"

"I don't know."

"Let me see your foot."

Tommy grabbed a fistful of Logan's jean and balanced on one leg while he lifted the other. The bottom of his foot was as black as the ink hospitals used on newborns to take their footprints.

"Can I have candy?" Tommy asked.

Logan didn't know if Sadie allowed the boys to eat candy, so he played it safe. "No candy. You'll get your sugar fix with the doughnuts." They stopped at the pastry display next to the soda machine. "What kind do you like?"

"I like 'em all."

"We'll get a couple of each." He filled two bags with a dozen and a half doughnuts, then grabbed four bottles of milk from the refrigerator and set their purchases on the checkout counter. "How's it going, Elmer?" The elderly man had worked at the Valero for the past five years.

"Where'd you pick up your friend?" Elmer smiled at Tommy.

Tommy spoke first. "How much money did the tooth fairy give you?"

Elmer's sagging jowls swallowed his chin. "What are you talkin' about, kid?"

"The tooth fairy leaves a dollar under my pillow for my tooth."

Elmer flashed his empty gums. "I didn't get nothin'."

"Why not?"

"'Cause I got my front teeth knocked out in a bar fight and I never did find them."

Tommy stepped on the candy shelf in front of the checkout and hoisted himself onto the counter. "You shoulda wrote the tooth fairy a note like my mom did."

Elmer scratched his balding head. "You don't say?"

"I lost my tooth at recess and I couldn't find it, but my mom wrote a note and the tooth fairy still came."

"Next time one of my teeth gets knocked out of my mouth, I'll give that a try," Elmer said.

"My mom can write you a note. She writes good notes."

Elmer chuckled and rang up the doughnuts and milk, then Logan slid his debit card through the machine.

"My mom's good at lots of stuff 'cause my dad doesn't live with us. He's moving to Balkimore."

Elmer's fuzzy eyebrows fused together over his nose.

Logan scooped his yappy partner off the counter, then handed him one of the pastry-filled bags. "Have a good day, Elmer." He opened the door for Tommy and they left the store.

"Can I eat a doughnut in the car?" Tommy asked after Logan buckled him into the booster seat.

Logan's brother and sister-in-law wouldn't appreciate him gifting them a dirty car seat, but faced with the prospect of Tommy's chatter all the way back to the motel he decided to take his chances and keep the kid's mouth busy chewing rather than talking. "Go ahead and have a doughnut."

The only noise on the return ride was the country music playing on the radio. As the pickup approached the motel a few minutes later, Logan spotted Sadie standing outside her room, arms crossed, her flip-flop tapping the cement. As soon as she saw the pickup, she marched across the parking lot, her blond hair swaying in rhythm with her hips.

"I think we're in trouble, buddy." He glanced in the rearview mirror. Tommy's cheeks were puffed out like a chipmunk's.

"What happened?" he asked, giving Logan an eyeful of pulverized doughnut and raspberry filling.

"I don't think your mother's happy we took off without her." Sadie wasn't dressed to go anywhere in a nightshirt that ended just above her knees. The baggy material did nothing to conceal her figure and Logan couldn't help appreciating her womanly curves.

Logan shifted into Park and pulled the key from the ignition, all the while keeping his gaze on Sadie. He doubted she had any idea that he could see the shadow of her bikini panties and the outline of her breasts beneath the blue shirt. He forced himself to look away from the bouncing temptation. "C'mon, kid. Time to face the music." He hopped out and opened the back door, then helped Tommy to the ground.

"Thomas James McHenry." Sadie cornered her son against the side of the truck. "You know you're never supposed to wander off without telling me."

Tommy's eyes crossed as he watched his mother's finger wag in front of his nose.

Then her finger pointed at the ground. "Where are your shoes?"

Tommy dropped his gaze and stared at his feet as if he expected his toes to answer his mother.

"And you—" Sadie glared at Logan. "How could you just take off with my son and not tell me first?"

"I left a note on the—"

"I don't care about a note." Sadie's voice rose in pitch and Logan worried that she'd wake the guests in the other rooms. "We may be distantly related now, but I hardly know you and my sons don't know you at all."

"Mom." Tommy tugged on Sadie's shirt. "How come you're yelling at Uncle Logan?"

Sadie ignored her son but lowered her voice. "It's inexcusable that you drove Tommy somewhere without securing him in his booster seat."

Logan doubted Sadie would allow him to get a word in edgewise if he tried to defend himself, so he reached behind Tommy and opened the pickup door.

Sadie's eyes widened. "Where did—"

"I bought it for Gunner and Lydia's baby. It's top-of-the-line. Fits newborns and older kids."

She rubbed her brow before looking him in the eye. "I'm sorry I yelled at you, but I panicked when I woke and Tommy wasn't in bed with Tyler." She ruffled Tommy's hair. "This guy has wandered off before and each time I lose ten years off my life."

"I'm sorry. I should have waited until you'd woken and asked permission to take him with me." His apology earned him a half smile from Sadie.

"Mom?"

"What?"

"Can you write a note to the tooth fairy?"

The question caught Sadie off guard and she lowered her finger. "What?"

"Elmo lost his teeth, but he can't find them and he needs a note so the tooth fairy can give him two dollars."

"Elmer," Logan corrected, keeping a straight face. "Not Elmo."

"Mom?"

"What?"

"Uncle Logan bought us doughnuts." Tommy held up the bag.

"I see that." Her gaze shifted to Logan. "When did he leave the room this morning?"

"A little after five thirty, I found him playing on the swings."

"I told Uncle Logan you said we could have doughnuts for breakfast," Tommy said.

"There isn't a doughnut shop in Stampede, so we drove down to the Valero. Elmer works in the convenience store."

"Mom?"

"What?"

"I gotta pee."

"Go!" Sadie pointed to their motel room and Tommy took off running. "That boy will be the death of me yet."

"Where's Tyler?"

"Still sleeping." Her gaze followed Tommy across the lot. "Or he was."

Tyler stood in the open doorway, rubbing sleep from his eyes.

Right then Gunner stepped from room 1, wearing only his boxers. "What's all the commotion out here?"

His gaze traveled over Sadie, then he looked at Logan and grinned. "You get lucky last night, big brother?"

OH. MY. GOD.

Sadie crossed her arms over her chest, hoping to hide her unharnessed boobs. She'd been in such a panic when she woke up, and after finding Logan's note on the door, she'd forgotten she was wearing only a pair of panties and a flimsy nightshirt. This was not how she'd planned to dress when she saw Lydia and Gunner this morning. Before Sadie found her voice, squealing tires startled her. Logan grasped her arm and stepped in front of her, shielding her from view. An old pickup that looked like it had been unearthed from a junkyard turned into the motel and veered toward the office. A minute later, Aunt Amelia's 1958 white Thunderbird convertible pulled alongside the clunker.

"We've got trouble," Logan said.

"What's going on?" she asked.

"Just watch. You'll see."

Aunt Amelia got out of her car and marched toward the jalopy, unaware of the onlookers. "Emmett Hardell, you are the orneriest man alive."

Logan's grandfather hitched his pants, then balled his hands into fists. "I let you run roughshod over me once, but I'm done playing party to your foolish ideas."

Amelia spread her arms wide. "Look at this motel. There are five vehicles parked in the lot. If you believe making money is foolish, then maybe you should spend your final days hiding under a rock."

"Oh, dear," Sadie whispered.

"Wait. It'll get better." Logan reached behind him

and brushed his fingers against the back of Sadie's hand, his warm touch distracting her.

"If I could find a rock right now, I'd—"

"Grandpa." Gunner approached the elderly couple. "I thought you two kissed and made up."

Lydia had told Sadie and Scarlett that their wealthy aunt had been feuding with Emmett Hardell, the mayor of Stampede, over her desire to revitalize the town and she'd finally taken matters into her owns hands. Apparently Amelia had another idea up her sleeve after she'd convinced Emmett to spruce up his motel.

"If I didn't know better," Gunner said, strutting forward, "I'd think all this arguing is nothing more than foreplay."

Sadie sucked in a quick breath.

"You watch your mouth, grandson." Emmett glared at Gunner.

"Lydia said they dated in high school." Sadie peered around Logan's broad shoulder.

"We can't figure it out," Logan said. "One second they like each other and the next they're scratching each other's eyes out."

Emmett pointed at Amelia. "She's up to her old shenanigans again."

Aunt Amelia raised her hands and lifted her face to the sky as if God would save her from the geezer. "I'm trying to better this town."

"I let you talk me into fixing up a perfectly good motel and now you want me to put some stupid tourist attraction on my ranch."

"People need something to do when they visit Stampede."

Emmett jabbed his finger in the air. "We don't need

strangers running loose kicking up more dust in this town."

Sadie was so focused on the arguing couple that she didn't notice Tommy had walked up to the pair until her son patted Emmett's leg.

"If I yell," Tommy said, "I have to sit in a time-out."

Amelia smiled. "What's your name, young man?"

"Tommy." He pointed at the last motel room. "That's Tyler. We're twins."

"Oh my goodness." Amelia pressed her hand to her chest and looked at Emmett. "These are Sadie's boys."

"Hello, Aunt Amelia." Sadie waved, her face burning as if she'd left her glycolic facial mask on too long.

The door to room 1 opened and Tommy shouted, "Aunt Lydia!" He raced over to her and she bent to hug him.

"Hey, kiddo, it's great to see you." Lydia glanced down the sidewalk, and when she saw Tyler hanging out in front of room 6, she smiled and said, "Come give me a hug, Tyler." He ran into Lydia's arms. "I've missed you guys." She took their hands and walked over to Gunner. "This is your uncle Gunner. He and I are married now."

"Who's Tommy and who's Tyler? I can't tell you guys apart," Gunner said.

"That's 'cause we're twins." Tommy looked at his brother. "Right?"

Tyler's head bobbed.

"We didn't expect you until later today." Aunt Amelia looked at Sadie.

"I decided to drive straight through, but we didn't get in until after midnight." She offered Emmett an apologetic smile and crossed her arms in front of her.

"This morning Tommy left the room without telling me and then—"

"It's my fault," Logan said. "Tommy woke before the others and we drove down to the Valero to buy doughnuts without telling Sadie."

Gunner whistled low between his teeth and Logan shot him a dirty look before he spoke to the boys. "Hey, Tyler, come over here and get something to eat." He reached into the truck for the bag of doughnuts and then opened the caps on the milk bottles and handed them to the boys.

"I can't believe how much they've grown." Amelia clapped her hands and smiled. "And they're talking in full sentences now."

Lydia visibly struggled not to laugh. "How long are you staying in town, Sadie?"

Couldn't the details wait until she was dressed? "I haven't decided."

Amelia glanced at the boys, who sat on the ground, licking their sticky fingers. "Lydia said Peter decided to move to Baltimore with his girlfriend."

Sadie didn't want to air her problems in front of Logan and his family. "We'll talk about it later."

"You never did tell me the reason for your spur-of-the-moment decision to visit Stampede." Her aunt refused to drop the subject.

Sadie might as well come clean. She curled her toes against her rubber flip-flops and said, "I lost my job."

Lydia's gasp echoed in Sadie's ears, but it was Logan's warm look of sympathy that reached deep inside her and hugged her heart. In the space of fifteen minutes this man had angered, frustrated and annoyed her, yet right now as she gazed into his eyes, she couldn't remember why. She felt her body sway toward him, as if she trusted he would steady her from the inside out.

"What happened?" Aunt Amelia asked.

It took all of Sadie's willpower to break eye contact with Logan. "I'd prefer to have clothes on before we discuss this."

Her aunt's eyes widened as if she'd just realized Sadie wore a nightshirt. Amelia looked at Emmett. "Expect a visit later this afternoon from me and Sadie."

"What for?" Emmett said.

"If I tell you, you'll run off and hide." Amelia nodded to Logan. "Make sure your grandfather stays put at the ranch until we arrive."

"Aunt Amelia," Sadie said. "I have the boys and—"

"Lydia will watch the twins. They can play in the attic while we're gone," Amelia said.

"I have an appointment with a client this afternoon, Aunt Amelia," Lydia said.

Aware of everyone's eyes on her, Sadie caved in. "The boys will have to come with us, then." She could only hope Tommy didn't stir up trouble.

Emmett grumbled under his breath, then glared at Amelia. "Is this a one coffeepot or two coffeepot visit?"

"Two," Amelia said. "But make it strong because you might not like my idea."

Emmett climbed behind the wheel, shut the door, then poked his head out the open window. "When have I ever liked one of your ideas?" He turned the key in the ignition and the engine backfired. Amelia jumped, then smacked her hand against the pickup's tailgate before getting into her car.

The old people drove off, turning their vehicles in opposite directions when they entered the highway. Sadie looked at Lydia. "Will you please watch the kids while I change clothes?"

"Of course." Lydia joined the boys on the ground and helped herself to a doughnut.

Sadie had been on autopilot since losing her job, and not until this very moment—while she stood with her hair a snarled mess, wearing an unflattering nightshirt and no makeup in front of a handsome single man—did her resolve waver. Tears burned her eyes and she knew if she didn't walk away right then, she'd break down. With a curt nod she strode back to the Stagecoach room, wishing she could jump on John Wayne's horse and ride into a sunset all by herself.

Chapter Three

"She looks mean," Tommy said late Saturday afternoon.

Logan studied Sweet Pea and tried to see the mare through the eyes of a three-and-a-half-foot-tall four-year-old. "Why does she look mean?"

The kid ignored the question and kicked the pile of hay next to the stall, sending the feed flying into the air. Distracted by the dried grass fluttering to the ground, he jumped around, trying to catch the bits and pieces in his hands.

"What do you think, Tyler?" The boy hadn't spoken since he and his brother arrived at the ranch with their mother and Amelia fifteen minutes ago. Logan had returned from delivering hay to the cattle just in time to entertain the twins while Gramps and the women gathered in the kitchen to discuss Amelia's latest wacky idea.

Tyler remained silent and he didn't press the boy to speak. Logan had been drawn to the brothers the moment he'd met them. He'd always anticipated being a dad, but fatherhood wasn't in the cards for him. When he'd had to quit rodeoing and returned home to run the ranch, he'd missed interacting with the children who traveled the circuit with their fathers.

Logan didn't badger Tyler into talking. Instead he asked, "Who wants to feed Sweet Pea a carrot?"

Tommy walked off and climbed onto the hay bales in the corner. Logan looked at Tyler, whose gaze remained on the horse. After a few seconds he said, "She looks sad."

Startled, he studied the mare. "You're probably right. A few weeks ago her best friend went away." Ranger had been twenty-eight and had developed a tumor that put pressure on his heart. The vet had had to put him down.

Tyler's brows scrunched in concentration. "Is her friend gonna come back?"

"No, he isn't." A sliver of guilt pricked Logan. He should pay more attention to the mare, but when did he have time? He was the only one who did any work around the ranch. Gunner was busy running the motel and fixing up Emmylou Schmidt's downtown antiques shop, which Amelia had purchased for Lydia as a wedding gift. They'd converted the lower floor into an office for Lydia's interior design business and were turning the upper floor into an apartment.

That left his middle brother to help Logan, and Reid sure in heck wasn't going to leave New Mexico to muck stalls. The thousand dollars Reid sent to their grandfather every month was guilt money, but Logan couldn't figure out what his brother had to feel remorseful about.

"I think Sweet Pea could use a friend," Logan said.

Tyler's blue eyes blinked at Logan. "I can be her friend."

"How about you climb up that ladder—" Logan

pointed across the aisle "—and I'll bring Sweet Pea out of her stall so you can rub her nose. She likes that."

Logan checked to make sure Tommy wasn't getting into trouble at the back of the barn, then he set Tyler on the ladder. "Sit back so your butt sticks through the opening." Tyler obeyed. "Are you wedged in there nice and tight?" Another nod. "Don't move."

Logan walked Sweet Pea out of her stall and brought her to stand before Tyler. "Touch her like this." Logan stroked the mare's nose.

When Tyler rubbed Sweet Pea's face, the horse snuffled the front of the kid's shirt. "She's soft."

"Can I have a turn?" Tommy tugged on the back pocket of Logan's jeans.

"Wait over there until I tell you to come closer." He didn't want the boy to get kicked by a horse, or to have to explain to Sadie how he'd let it happen.

Tyler leaned forward and wrapped his arms around Sweet Pea's neck, resting his cheek against her face. The tender scene yanked Logan's heartstrings.

"Do you boys have any pets at home?" he asked.

"Mom says we can't have a dog," Tommy answered. "'Cause she's gotta work and it costs a lot of money."

Logan and his brothers had grown up with dogs, barn cats, horses, chickens and even a pet raccoon that took up residence beneath the shed behind the house. Their last hound dog, Blue, had died several years ago, and when Logan had asked his grandfather if he wanted to get another dog from the shelter, the old man had declined, arguing that he wouldn't be around long enough to take care of the mutt.

Gramps acted as if death was knocking at his door, but Gunner believed their grandfather was too ornery to ever die. When Amelia Rinehart had begun her campaign to resurrect Stampede, Logan and his brother had seen a change in their grandfather. He was still a grumpy old man, but he had more get-up-and-go and was determined to contest the older woman in all manner of ways.

Tommy patted Logan's leg. "Is it my turn?"

Logan set Tyler on the ground behind him, then lifted Tommy into his arms and held him by Sweet Pea's head. After petting the horse twice, the boy said, "I'm bored."

Logan placed Tommy on his feet and returned the mare to her stall. "I promised Tyler he could read in the hayloft." Logan nodded to the ladder. "When you reach the top, keep away from the edge."

"I wanna see the hayloft," Tommy said.

Logan followed the boys up the ladder.

Tommy walked around the space. "How come it's full of hay?"

"The hay is for the horses and the cattle to eat." Logan pulled the string hanging from a naked lightbulb. "Do you think this is a cool place to read, Tyler?"

The boy nodded.

"What else can we do up here?" Tommy asked.

"Not much, I'm afraid. While Tyler reads, you can help me muck stalls." Tyler stared at the bales Logan had stacked in the shape of a giant chair. "You want me to toss your backpack up here?" Logan asked.

Tyler nodded.

Logan helped Tommy down the ladder, then walked to the barn entrance, where the boys had tossed their backpacks aside. He grabbed the one with the image of the dog on the front. "Stand back so you don't get hit." Logan flung the bag into the loft. "Holler when you're ready to come down and I'll help you." Logan had fond memories of playing in the hayloft as a kid. As soon as he and his brothers were old enough to climb the ladder, their grandfather had let them hang out in the barn while he'd taken care of the horses.

"How do you muck stalls?" Tommy asked.

"You'll see." The boy dogged Logan's heels as they left the barn. "First, you're going to sit on the corral rail and watch me bring the horses out." He plopped Tommy down. "After that we take the wheelbarrow and—"

"What's a wheelbarrow?"

"You'll see." The only way to spare himself the twenty-question game was to tire the kid out, but Logan knew from personal experience that boys like Tommy were never tired out.

THIS WAS NOT how Sadie anticipated spending her first day in Stampede. She and her aunt sat at Emmett's kitchen table while he stood at the counter with his back to them, waiting for the coffee to finish brewing—obviously not happy at having to play host to an afternoon coffee klatch.

At eighty-five, Emmett was the same age as Sadie's aunt, but he looked older. His shoulders sloped toward the ground as if life's problems had piled on year after year, weighing him down. Decades of ranching had etched deep crevices across the back of his neck and marked his arms with scaly sunspots.

Sadie surreptitiously studied her aunt. Blue veins crisscrossed the back of her hands, but unlike Emmett's leathery skin, Amelia's appeared pearlescent beneath the box light in the ceiling.

During the drive to Paradise Ranch, Aunt Amelia had rambled on about how developers had built single-family-home subdivisions north of the towns of Mesquite and Rocky Point. Stampede was too far away for those families to shop. And with a population that had never exceeded three thousand—even in its heyday—the dusty hidey-hole needed to find a way to survive or it would become nothing more than a ghost town. Which, apparently, was exactly what the old-timers who'd elected Emmett mayor wanted. When Sadie had asked why her aunt hadn't sought someone else's help to carry out her plans, she'd grown misty-eyed and said she was trying to involve Emmett because he'd been in a funk for such a long time.

This past summer, Lydia told Sadie that their aunt and Emmett had dated in high school. Sadie couldn't help wondering if Amelia still carried a torch for the old man and all this fuss over the town was just a ploy to get his attention. Feeling a need to break the silence, she said, "I like that rooster cookie jar on the counter, Emmett."

"I gave that to Emmett's wife, Sara, for her birthday years ago," Amelia said.

"Lydia said you and Sara were best friends." And that Sara had died of cancer when the Hardell boys were still in middle school.

The coffeemaker dinged and Emmett delivered three mugs of hot brew to the table. Then he sat and engaged Amelia in a glare-down. Neither said a word. This meeting had better kick into high gear because Sadie didn't want to leave Logan in charge of the boys for too long. She wasn't worried about Tyler getting into mischief, but—as Logan had discovered earlier—Tommy was adventuresome.

This morning wasn't the first time her son had wandered off. Once at preschool he'd escaped the playground through an open gate. Thankfully another parent had spotted him in the parking lot and had brought him inside. Although she hadn't been happy with Logan's decision to take her son to the convenience store without telling her, she gave credit where credit was due—he didn't know about Tommy's ADD, yet he'd had the common sense not to let her son out of his sight. If anyone was at fault, it was Sadie—she'd slept through the noise of Tommy opening all the locks on the motel room door. "Maybe I should check on the twins," she said.

"The boys are fine." Amelia sipped her coffee, then said, "I thought about building a town square after the motel was renovated, but I changed my mind when Walter Franklin called me."

"You cozying up to the bank president now?" Emmett looked at Sadie. "Your great-aunt's fortune keeps the bank's doors open, so she thinks she has the right to stick her nose into everyone's business."

Amelia ignored his barb. "Walter says you've fallen behind on the ranch mortgage."

Emmett's spine snapped straight. "What are you talking about?"

"The bank is ready to foreclose on your property."

"Walter's got no right sharing my personal business with you."

"He's concerned, Emmett. He knows Sara and I were close and the three of us go way back."

"Logan handles the ranch accounts. He hasn't said a word to me."

"The bank sent late-payment statements in April, May and June."

"Logan would have said something to me if he'd gotten them."

"Maybe he did and you forgot," Amelia said.

Emmett glared. "You think I'm addled now?"

Sadie held her breath when her aunt leaned forward, fingers curling as if she wanted to choke him. "If I thought your brain was stuck in some mental mud, I'd suggest building a sanatorium on your property instead of a tourist attraction."

"Why didn't Walter come out here and tell me?"

"Don't you remember? Walter was traveling through Europe all summer. The manager who took his place drove down from Dallas once a week and stayed only long enough to make sure the bank hadn't burned down before leaving again."

Emmett shook his head. "Doesn't make sense."

"Walter made calls on your behalf, but the bank refuses to give any concessions. You have thirty days to come up with the cash or you'll lose the ranch," Amelia said.

The sip of coffee Emmett gulped must have slid down the wrong pipe, because he fell into a coughing fit.

Amelia leaped from her chair and pounded his back. "Quit hacking or you'll break your ribs." Her aunt's hand went from whacking to rubbing in slow circles. Emmett's eyes drifted closed, then a moment later popped open.

"Quit slappin' me, Mimi."

Mimi? Where had that nickname come from? When Sadie's grandmother was alive, she'd never called her older sister Mimi.

"This is some cockamamy plot you and Walter conjured up so you could get your hands on my land."

Amelia sucked in a quick breath. "Don't be an ass. I would never conspire to steal Paradise Ranch out from under you." She sat down and lowered her voice. "I'm willing to pay off your debt."

"There is no debt until Logan says so," Emmett said.

"I knew you'd be stubborn—" Amelia nodded to Sadie. "That's why my niece is here."

"What's she got to do with you and Walter scheming against me?"

"Sadie has an accounting degree. Let her examine the ranch books. If the bank made a mistake, she'll find it."

Emmett drummed his knobby fingers against the tabletop. "You aren't offering her services out of the goodness of your heart. What's the catch?"

"If Walter's correct, I'll take care of the delinquent payments."

Emmett squinted. "In exchange for what?"

"For you agreeing to give up twenty-five acres of your property."

His lips parted and his breath escaped his mouth in a loud whoosh. "What are you going to do with twenty-five acres?"

"I plan to build a tourist attraction that you, Logan and Gunner will manage."

Amelia sipped her coffee and winced.

Emmett's mouth twitched. "Too strong for you?"

Sadie's aunt glared.

"What kind of tourist attraction?" Emmett asked.

"I want to use the acreage for trail rides and a petting zoo."

The coffee mug halted halfway to his lips, then returned to the table in slow motion.

"Before you tell me to jump in a lake, let me explain." Amelia held up one finger. "First, you don't have to invest a dime of your own money. I'll pick up the entire tab. Second—" another finger popped up "—everyone knows the land bordering the Los Lobos Ranch is useless rocky terrain, which makes it perfect for trail riding." A third finger appeared. "A petting zoo will interest families with children." Four fingers wiggled in front of his face. "And the attractions will bring in extra income for you and your grandsons."

Emmett didn't say a word and Amelia pushed harder. "Gunner and Lydia have a child on the way. Wouldn't you like to start a college fund for them?"

Her aunt had left off the fifth reason, but Sadie could guess what it was—Amelia hoped having to cater to tourists would breathe life back into her old flame.

"What do you think?" Amelia asked.

"You know what I think. It stinks," he said.

Her aunt crossed her arms over her chest. "Stampede would be the first town in the area to offer trail rides and a petting zoo. Rocky Point and Mesquite don't have anything similar."

"If you're bored, find a new hobby and stop messing with Stampede," he said.

"You can't afford to be your stubborn self—not when the ranch is at stake." Amelia drew in a deep breath. "This is a win-win situation. Paradise Ranch stays in your possession and brings in added income, and the town has a new tourist attraction."

"What man in his right mind would agree to turn his ranch into a three-ring circus?"

Amelia's face softened. "A man on the verge of losing what he'd hoped to keep in his family for generations to come."

Emmett's cheeks drooped as the reality of his situation sank in. "I guess it wouldn't hurt to let your niece have a look at the books."

"Aunt Amelia." Sadie jumped into the conversation. "Reviewing the finances of a large ranch will take hours or even days, and I have the boys to think about." The twins were too much for her aunt to handle for more than a couple of hours at a time.

"We'll figure out what to do with Tyler and Tommy later," Amelia said.

Emmett nodded to Sadie. "Logan will have to show you where everything is. I don't go into the office much anymore."

It was one thing to have a grumpy old man breathing down her neck while she pored over bank statements and ledgers, and another to have a handsome man close to her age watching her every move.

Emmett got up from the table and walked outside. As soon as the door closed behind him, Amelia clapped her hands together. "That went well, don't you think?"

"I'm not comfortable prying into Emmett's finances." Besides, her trip to Stampede was supposed to be a chance for her and the boys to catch their breath and spend time together while she figured out her next steps.

"Nonsense." Amelia walked to the door. "With your experience it won't take long to uncover the truth, and then Emmett will have no choice but to go along with my plan."

"I apologize if I'm stepping out of line," Sadie said. "But it's not like you to bully someone, and Emmett doesn't want you digging around in his private affairs."

"I may have come on a little strong, but it's for his own good."

"You still have feelings for him, don't you?"

Amelia pressed her hand over her heart. "I've never stopped caring for Emmett, not even when I was married to Robert."

Back in the day, Emmett and their aunt had broken up after an argument. A few days later Uncle Robert, an oil executive, had passed through Stampede on business and had swept Amelia off her feet.

"Let's find out what time Logan will be available to help you in the office tomorrow."

Sadie followed her aunt out the door and they cut across the yard. The sound of laughter met their ears as they approached the barn and they paused in the doorway to take in the scene.

Emmett sat on a hay bale in a corner next to Tyler, grinning as he watched Logan trot down the center of the barn pushing a wheelbarrow with Tommy seated inside. At the end of the aisle Logan applied the brakes and her son catapulted through the air and disappeared into a gigantic pile of hay. A moment later his head popped into view and he gasped for air between giggles.

"I want a turn!" Tyler shouted.

Sadie gaped in astonishment. Tyler hadn't smiled since Pete said his goodbyes and left town.

"Give the other young'un a turn," Emmett said.

Her aunt stepped forward, but Sadie grasped her arm and pulled her back into the shadows, then pressed a finger against her lips.

"That was cool, Uncle Logan!" Tommy crawled out of the hay.

Logan set Tyler in the barrow and backpedaled down the aisle, then said, "Ready?"

Tyler nodded.

"Go, Tyler!" Tommy yelled when Logan took off running. Tyler flew into the hay just like his brother had, his giggles warming Sadie's heart.

"Your turn." Tommy yanked Emmett's shirtsleeve.

"I'm too old for that nonsense."

Tommy tugged harder. "It's fun!"

Aunt Amelia's mouth dropped open when Emmett said, "Maybe I'll give it a try."

"Look out, Gramps wants a turn," Logan said.

Tyler walked over to Tommy's side and both boys planted their hands against Emmett's backside and pushed him forward. "Don't be afraid, Gramps," Tyler said. "You won't get hurt."

Sadie's throat grew tight when Tyler called Emmett "Gramps."

"You think you can push me?" Emmett asked Logan.

"Uncle Logan's got big muscles. He can push you," Tommy said.

Sadie's eyes skimmed over Uncle Logan and agreed that he looked plenty strong enough.

Logan helped his grandfather climb into the wheelbarrow. Once the old man was seated with his knees pulled up to his chest, Logan spoke. "You boys want to help me push?"

Tommy stood on Logan's right, Tyler on his left, both grasping the handle behind Logan's grip. "On the count of three," he said. "One…two…three!" They took off running.

"The old fool is going to break his neck," Amelia whispered.

Emmett went flying face-first and landed with his butt sticking up in the air. The boys jumped in after him, pushing the hay away from his head.

"Was it fun?" Tommy asked.

Emmett chortled, his chest shaking. Sadie watched her aunt's lips curve in a soft smile—she definitely had a crush on the old man.

"Give Gramps another ride!" Tommy and Tyler helped Emmett stand.

Amelia cleared her throat loudly and stepped out of the shadows.

"Busted," Logan said.

"Mom! Did you see what Uncle Logan did? He gave us a ride in a—" Tommy looked at Logan. "What's it called?"

"Wheelbarrow."

Tyler ran up to Sadie. "I got to read in the hayloft."

Sadie locked gazes with Logan. "Who knew barns could be so much fun?"

Logan's gaze dropped to Sadie's mouth and remained there too long to be considered a casual glance. "I better get back to work."

"What time should Sadie return tomorrow?" Amelia asked.

Logan nodded to his grandfather. "What's going on?"

"Amelia's niece is gonna look over the ranch books," Emmett said.

Sadie couldn't be sure the shadows in the barn weren't playing tricks with her eyes, but she swore Logan's face grew pale. "I don't understand."

"I'll explain later," Emmett said. "When's a good time you can help Sadie in the office?"

Logan rubbed his gloved hands down the front of his pants. "Late afternoon."

"Can I come, Mom?" Tommy said.

"Me, too," Tyler whispered, his eyes pleading.

"Not tomorrow, boys." A deafening "Pleeeeease" threatened to damage her eardrums.

"I'll watch the boys," Emmett said.

"Gramps can play with us." Tommy raced over to Emmett's side.

"What are we gonna do?"

"Don't be ridiculous. You can't keep up with two four-year-olds," Amelia said.

Emmett planted his knuckles on his slim hips. "I might have one foot in the grave, but I ain't dead yet."

"The twins can get a little wild, Emmett," Sadie said.

"We'll find something for them to do in the house." Logan studied Tyler, who stood by Sadie. Had he sensed her quiet son always paid a price for his brother's hyperactive behavior?

"Please, Mom," Tommy pleaded.

"Fine. You can come with me." If the boys got out of hand, she'd leave.

Amelia pointed at Emmett. "You better act your

age. The last thing you need is a broken hip." She left the barn.

"Boys, what do you say to your uncle Logan and… Gramps?"

"Thank you!" Tommy yelled, then raced after Amelia.

Tyler walked over to Logan. "I liked the hayloft."

"You're welcome to read up there anytime I'm working in the barn."

Tyler hugged Logan's muscular thigh, then chased after his brother. It was probably the dust motes floating in the air or a sudden allergy to hay that caused Sadie's eyes to water. "See you tomorrow." She fled the barn, blinking until her vision cleared.

The realization that her sons' father had for all intents and purposes abandoned them when he'd moved out of state had hit her hard when Tyler hugged Logan. The only family members actively involved in her and the boys' lives anymore were their aunts, and—now that Lydia had moved to Stampede—it was just her and Scarlett living in Madison.

Sadie had intended to focus her attention on the boys during their visit to Stampede, but after seeing how they'd gravitated toward Emmett and Logan, she had a hunch it was male attention they craved more than their mother fussing over them. She was grateful to the Hardell men for being kind to the twins and could only hope that when it was time to say goodbye, the boys wouldn't feel abandoned all over again.

Chapter Four

Sunday morning Logan parked his pickup at the northern end of the property. He grabbed the fence stretcher, pliers and leather gloves before hiking up the incline to tighten a section of sagging barbed wire. He'd been working since 5:00 a.m., but six hours of nonstop physical labor had done nothing to loosen the knot of anxiety in the pit of his stomach.

Yesterday, after Sadie and Amelia had left the ranch with the twins, his grandfather had given Logan the bad news. *Foreclosure* was a swear word and synonymous with doomsday in any ranching dictionary.

Last night he'd lain awake, racking his brain to come up with a good enough reason for failing to pay the mortgage three months in a row. A severe thunderstorm in April had made a mess of the ranch, and Logan had been forced to hire a crew to remove the fallen trees. The service hadn't been cheap. In May the engine in Gramp's truck had died. He'd forked over cash to have the pickup towed to an auto-repair shop, where a mechanic had practically rebuilt the engine. Then at the beginning of June the septic tank had backed up. The system was twenty-five years old and P. U. Septic Services claimed it would cost almost as much to repair it as replace it, so the ranch now had a brand-new state-of-the-art septic system. The only excuse Logan could come up with was that he'd mistakenly assumed he'd paid the mortgage when he'd seen the low balance in the checking account. Until this latest disaster, his inability to focus and keep track of things hadn't caused any major financial consequences.

Back in March he'd consulted a doctor about his trouble concentrating and the physician had diagnosed him with ADD. He'd been given a prescription for Ritalin, but the pills had caused insomnia and after a month of grogginess and overdosing on coffee he'd quit taking the medication. The doctor then recommended Logan consider cognitive behavioral therapy, but who had time to attend a two-hour session two days a week? He could have asked Gunner to help with the ranch chores when he had to leave town, but stubborn pride had kept him from sharing his diagnosis with his family. Logan was the eldest grandson. He was supposed to be able to handle things. It was his job to take care of others, not vice versa.

After the diagnosis, depression had settled in and managing the ranch had become a greater struggle. Each morning he woke up with a mile-long to-do list in his head, so he'd begun jotting reminders to himself on paper. But inevitably, he'd lose the note or find it three days later in a jeans pocket when he did laundry.

Logan set his tools on the ground and shoved his hands into a pair of work gloves. He had to find a way out of this jam without having to accept Amelia's money in exchange for handing over twenty-five acres of land to Amelia Rinehart. As much as he wasn't looking forward to appearing like an idiot in front of Sadie, if she could wade through the mess he'd made of the finances, he'd gladly play the fool.

A horn blast caught his attention. Gunner's pickup parked next to Logan's truck. His brother hiked up the hill. "Gramps said the bank's after the ranch. What's going on?"

"We missed a few payments," Logan said.

"We? You're supposed to be taking care of the bills."

Logan squeezed the pliers to keep from banging them against his brother's forehead. Paying the bills hadn't been part of the deal when Logan had agreed to retire from rodeo and return home to care for the cattle. But Gramps had run out of steam, and before Logan knew it, he'd begun fetching the mail every day and spending his nights sorting through bills and invoices and cutting checks. The stress had only grown worse when Logan and his new wife had tried to start a family and discovered that he was sterile. It wasn't long after that Beth had filed for divorce. He'd hit rock bottom for a while and it had been all he could do to haul his butt out of bed at dawn to feed the cattle. "I am taking care of the bills."

"Gramps said Sadie's coming out this afternoon to look over the accounts."

"Give me a hand." Logan inserted the wire loop into one end of the stretcher and waited for Gunner to make another loop from the roll of barbed wire he'd brought with him.

"What have you been doing with the money Reid sends home every month?" Gunner asked.

Logan pulled the wire taut with the stretcher. "I've

been putting the checks into a separate savings account for Gramps."

"Why don't you use that money to cover the missed mortgage payments?"

"That nest egg is earmarked for when the time comes that Gramps needs extra care." Their grandfather deserved as much after practically raising Logan and his brothers because their deadbeat parents hadn't cared about doing what was best for their kids.

When Gunner turned twenty-one, their grandfather had gone to the bank and put the ranch in his grandsons' names—so the state of Texas couldn't come after the land to pay for his care when he went into a nursing home. Logan hoped his grandfather would kick the bucket in his sleep, but if that didn't happen, he intended to use the savings to hire a visiting nurse to watch over Gramps so he could live out his final days at the ranch. Logan had planned it all out but hadn't anticipated that they might lose the place ahead of their grandfather's final days.

"There's another busted wire over here." Logan walked ten yards away.

"Lydia said you were goofing off with the twins in the barn yesterday."

"They're cute kids." After Beth had divorced him, Logan had come to terms with the fact that he'd never father any children and he'd coped with the pain by trying to convince himself that he didn't want to be a dad. But the fun he'd had with Tommy and Tyler had proved he was fooling himself.

Gunner cranked the fence stretcher until the wire grew taut. "Supposedly Sadie's ex is a real jerk. Late with his child support payments, and he can't hang on to a job for more than six months at a time."

Logan let his brother ramble on, eager to hear more about Lydia's pretty cousin. "I guess Sadie hasn't dated much since her divorce because guys run the opposite way after she tells them about the twins."

Maybe Logan should join an online dating site, and if he met someone special who already had children, he could be like a dad to them. Then again, once a woman saw how disorganized his life was, they'd want no part of it.

"I need to get back to the motel," Gunner said.

"Tell Gramps I'll be home—" Logan wiped his sleeve across his sweaty forehead "—after I check the water in the stock tanks."

"Sure thing." Gunner dropped the wire stretcher on the ground.

Logan watched his brother drive away, cursing the rotten luck that had made him the firstborn sibling. Then he cursed his mother and his ex-wife for leaving him because he wasn't perfect; his dead father, who'd spent his time on earth womanizing; and his grandfather, who had trouble controlling his drinking when he was left alone. And, finally, he cursed himself because he'd only been going through the motions the past six years since his divorce, busting his backside day in and day out, wondering what it was all for. It had taken a pretty woman and her twin sons to shake him up and make him admit that he wanted more for himself.

"Lydia, this is amazing." Sadie stood in the middle of Aunt Amelia's attic. "It's a true playroom now."

"Look, Mom!" Tommy sprinted across the carpet and sat at a vintage school desk.

"Your aunts and I used to practice our spelling words at those desks," Sadie said.

"Aunt Amelia was generous with her money, so I went a little overboard." Lydia nodded to a sailing trunk filled with costumes, which sat in front of a full-length ornate mirror attached to the wall. "I ordered most of the clothes online and made sure I included some pink tutus." She smiled. "Just in case."

"I hope you have a little girl." Sadie smiled at Tyler, who had crawled onto the padded bench beneath the stained-glass window. "You made a reading nook."

"Just for Tyler." Lydia walked over to a sideboard attached to the wall. "And because Tommy loves to build things, I filled these baskets with Lego bricks and building blocks."

Her cousin had thought of everything. "The boys have missed you," Sadie said.

"I missed them, too. It's crazy how life works, isn't it? I came down here to help Aunt Amelia with the motel and had no idea I'd find my perfect match in Stampede."

"What did your folks say when you told them you and Gunner were married and expecting a baby?"

Lydia rolled her eyes. "They were surprised, but you know how busy they are with the law firm. They sent us a nice check and said they'd visit at Thanksgiving. I'm hoping the apartment will be renovated by then."

"I'm glad you're happy here," Sadie said, "and our aunt loves having you around."

"Aunt Amelia made a fresh pitcher of lemonade

before she left for a meeting with the ladies' society this morning. We'll let the boys play and talk in the kitchen."

Sadie followed her cousin downstairs, where Lydia poured two glasses of lemonade and brought them to the table. Their aunt's brick Victorian was almost a hundred years old but had gone through several renovations throughout the years. The kitchen had been expanded to include a butcher-block island with seating for three. The gray-and-white counters and large farm sink complemented the white cupboards with glass-front doors. State-of-the-art appliances and a beautiful wood floor gave the space an updated appearance.

"How long will it stay this warm before there's a break in the temperature?" Sadie asked.

"Gunner said we could see ninety-degree temps on and off from now all the way through September." Lydia waved her hand. "Forget about the weather. Why didn't you tell me you lost your job before you came down here?"

"There was nothing you could have done."

"I bet you told Scarlett to keep your secret, but she's usually the one with the big mouth."

"I made her promise not to tell anyone in the family." Sadie pointed to Lydia's belly. "You said you were due in April. Do you have an exact due date?"

Lydia frowned. "Didn't I tell you?"

"Tell me what?"

"The doctor I'm seeing in Mesquite thinks the nurse at the clinic in Madison miscalculated my due date by a whole month."

"Seriously?"

"I'm due early March."

"That makes sense, then, with how much you're showing," Sadie said. "Maybe you should schedule an ultrasound just to be sure."

"I'll bring it up with the doctor at my next appointment."

"Have you decided on a name?" Sadie asked.

"Gunner thinks our child should have a Western name, but I don't want a son called Beau or a daughter named Pearl." Lydia changed the subject. "When are you going back to Madison?"

Sadie twirled her glass. "I don't have a game plan right now."

"What are you talking about?"

"Pete moved away, so there's no reason I have to rush back to Wisconsin. I can live off the severance pay I received for a few months."

"What about the boys' preschool?"

"I'm still paying the monthly tuition to keep their spots, but I've got Tommy on a waiting list to get into a program for kids with ADD. I definitely need to find a new job before the beginning of next year so I can afford to pay the tuition if he gets in."

"I thought you didn't want to separate the boys in school."

"I don't. But I want what's best for both of my sons, and if it means separating them while they're in preschool in order to help Tommy be better prepared for kindergarten, then we'll deal with it."

Lydia's eyes widened. "You and the boys should live here in Stampede."

"If I didn't have to worry about Tommy getting help for his ADD, I'd be tempted. I've always loved visiting Aunt Amelia." Sadie smiled. "When we spoke on the phone this summer, I heard something different in your voice. Fixing up the motel drove you crazy, but you always sounded upbeat and happy."

"It didn't take long for Gunner and Stampede to grow on me."

Sadie nodded. "I want more for my sons than living in an apartment with no yard. And spending all day in preschool before being bused to extracurricular activities because I can't pick them up until I get off work."

Lydia grasped Sadie's hand and squeezed. "You're doing the best you can for your sons."

But maybe she could do better. "The lease on our apartment would have been up September first, so I put our belongings in a storage unit, pulled the twins out of preschool and decided to spend time with you and Aunt Amelia."

"Gunner would love it if you moved here. Then he wouldn't have to tag along with me when I go flea-market shopping."

Since her cousin had brought up her husband, Sadie asked, "What do you know about Logan?"

Lydia's eyes sparkled and Sadie hoped her cousin wasn't assuming she was attracted to her brother-in-law, even though she was.

"Logan's divorced. Gunner says he doesn't talk about his breakup with Beth. They met on the rodeo circuit and got married right before Logan returned to Stampede to manage the ranch."

"Logan was a rodeo cowboy?"

Lydia nodded. "Gunner said he was pretty good and won a few buckles."

"Why did he give up rodeo?"

"When their father, Donny, died, Gunner had just

graduated from high school and Reid was in the military, so the responsibility for helping Emmett with the ranch fell on Logan's shoulders."

"Is Reid still in the military?"

Lydia shook her head. "After his enlistment was up, he moved to New Mexico and hasn't been home in a few years."

"Why's that?"

"Gunner has no idea. He texted Reid that we got married and we're expecting a baby, and his brother texted back *congratulations* and that was it."

"We used to complain about not having any siblings, but maybe we got off easy." Sadie, Lydia and Scarlett had been named after their grandmothers and Sadie always felt bad that Aunt Amelia would never have a granddaughter named after her. "Our family tree is boring compared to the Hardells'."

"Now that Gunner has warmed up to being a father he's already trying to talk me into having a large family."

Sadie had always planned on having three children— she'd just never expected two of them would be twins.

"It's funny how life works out. I can't imagine raising children with anyone but Gunner."

"I'm glad you two found each other." Sadie's stomach clenched with jealousy at the loving look in her cousin's eyes. Maybe one day she'd find a man she could feel the same way about.

"What are you doing at the ranch today?"

"Aunt Amelia twisted Emmett's arm into allowing me to review the accounts." Sadie rested her elbows on the table.

Lydia's phone beeped with a text message. She released a loud sigh.

"What is it?" Sadie asked.

"Gunner checks in with me every couple of hours to see if I'm feeling okay. He's going to drive me nuts by the time the baby arrives." She slung her purse over her shoulder. "I need to stop by the motel before I meet with the electrician at the apartment."

"See you later." Sadie glanced up at the kitchen ceiling. It sounded like a herd of elephants was running loose on the second floor. She took her empty glass to the sink, then went to the stairs in the front hall.

"Boys?"

Tommy appeared on the landing, his chest puffing from exertion. She pointed to his sock feet. "Why did you take your shoes off?"

"Watch how far I can slide." He ran out of sight. She heard his feet slap against the floor as he raced back to the stairs.

"Be careful." Sadie was halfway up the steps when Tommy slid into view. She expected him to stop before he reached the first step, but he lost his balance and went airborne. Sadie lunged forward and wrapped her arms around him. They tumbled, Sadie's back slamming against each step until they landed with a hard thud on the foyer floor.

Tommy scrambled off her, his eyes wide and frightened.

"I'm okay," she wheezed, her back burning as if someone held a blowtorch against her skin.

"Mom!" Tyler's voice came from the top of the stairs. He descended the steps, his hand clinging to the rail. When he reached her, tears welled in his eyes and he sank to his knees and rubbed her head.

Tommy's lower lip trembled and Sadie's heart ached for him. Her little torpedo was always causing trouble and now he'd hurt his mother. She lifted her hand and he grasped her fingers.

"I just need to catch my breath." She raised her other hand to Tyler. "Help me up."

They tugged on her arms and Sadie did her best not to wince at the sharp pain that raced across her shoulders. Thankfully she hadn't hit her head on the steps. "Go use the bathroom and don't forget to wash your hands. Then get your backpacks and we'll head out to the ranch."

Ten minutes later they piled into the minivan and Sadie checked to see that the boys had buckled themselves into their booster seats before she gingerly climbed behind the wheel and drove off. For a change, the twins were quiet—no doubt her fall had scared them as much as it had her. Fifteen minutes later she parked next to Emmett's pickup, but Logan's truck was missing.

She helped the boys out of the van, then locked the doors and stared at their cute faces. "Use your manners. This isn't our house, so we don't touch things without asking, okay?"

Their heads bobbed.

"Listen to Gramps and do what he says. Understood?"

"Can we go in the barn?" Tyler asked.

"Maybe later, after I finish working."

The front door opened and Emmett stepped outside. "Didn't expect you for another hour."

"The boys were restless," Sadie said, climbing the porch steps after the twins.

"Logan's out checking the cattle."

"If you show me to the office, I'm sure I can keep busy until he gets back."

Emmett turned away and the boys followed him inside, letting the door slam shut before Sadie reached it. When she entered the house, Emmett pointed to his left. "The office is in there." He disappeared down the hallway, the boys trailing him.

Sadie's gaze swung back and forth between the office door and the kitchen—she worried her sons would run circles around Logan's grandfather. The sound of clanging pots and pans propelled her toward the office. When she stepped inside, she gasped at the mess.

She closed her eyes, sure she'd imagined her first glimpse of the chaos inside the room. But when she lifted her eyelids, it still looked as if a bomb had exploded inside the space. A large desk sat against the far wall, the entire surface covered with papers, files, newspapers, coffee mugs and…a dirty sock?

Cheap bookcases made out of plywood stood on either side of the window. She perused the titles, covering ranching, horticulture, cattle and the history of Texas. A bright yellow cover snagged her attention—a gardening book. She flipped through the worn pages, discovering notes written in a feminine hand next to various photos.

Put in front of the porch had been written beneath a photo of a Knock Out rosebush. *Back door*, next to an image of a butterfly bush, and *plant along driveway*, by a picture of a pink crepe myrtle tree.

Sadie stared out the window overlooking the front

yard. The rosebushes looked anorexic. With only a handful of blooms they were starving for nutrients. The six crepe myrtle trees bordering the gravel drive needed to be cut back and thinned out. Yesterday when she and her aunt had walked to the barn, Sadie hadn't seen a butterfly bush anywhere in the backyard. She clutched the book to her chest. What would Emmett's wife think if she could see her beloved plants wasting away?

The office door opened, startling Sadie. She spun and came face-to-face with a sweaty, dusty, unsmiling Logan.

"You're early." His gaze darted around the room, pinging off objects with lightning speed. He reminded her of Tommy when he walked into his preschool room and didn't know which way to go first.

"The boys were getting antsy at Amelia's house." She nodded to the doorway behind him. "I doubt I'll have a lot of time before they grow bored and your grandfather turns them back over to me." Feeling like a cornered rabbit, she slid the garden book onto the shelf, then clasped her fingers together.

"I'll grab a quick shower, then we can get started." Like a man heading to his own execution, Logan skulked from the room, his boot heels clunking against the stairs, each loud *bang* protesting her presence in the house.

Chapter Five

Logan took his time showering and changing clothes. He knew it was rude to keep Sadie waiting, but what man was eager to look like a fool in front of a woman he found attractive? Especially when that pretty lady was his cousin-in-law?

When he returned downstairs, he paused in the foyer and listened to his grandfather and the twins—mostly Tommy—jabber about playing soccer. If he could come up with a fake emergency that would call him away from the house…

A loud crash in the office sent him running into the room, where he found Sadie on her knees by the desk.

"What happened?" He grasped her elbows and helped her to stand. Her eyes filled with tears. "Did you hurt yourself?"

"I'm fine." She drew in shallow breaths and placed a hand gingerly against her lower back.

"You're in pain." He moved her arm out of the way and lifted the hem of her T-shirt. "How did you get these marks?" The bruises and welts were fresh. Was this why she'd shown up in the middle of the night at the motel? Had she fled Wisconsin because her ex had hurt her?

"I fell." She tugged her shirt down.

"I'll get an ice pack." He turned but she grabbed his arm, her fingernails leaving half-moon marks on his skin.

"I'll be okay. I bumped the bruises when I bent over to pick up a file that fell off the desk."

It wasn't any of his business, but since she was about to stick her nose into his personal affairs… "Did your ex do this to you?"

Her eyes widened and she took a step back, her legs bumping into the chair. "Only a low-down miserable excuse for a man would hurt a woman," he said.

"My ex did not do this to me. My son did." She released a quiet sigh. "Tommy tumbled down the stairs at my aunt's house and I broke his fall."

"The bruises are swollen. I'll be right back." He went into the kitchen and took a bag of frozen peas out of the freezer.

"What are you doing with those?" his grandfather asked.

"Don't worry, I'm not eating them." Logan grabbed a dish towel off the counter. "Where are the boys?"

"On the porch shucking corn for the shepherd's pie I'm making for supper."

Logan peeked through the screen door and saw the kids having a sword fight with ears of corn.

"You and Sadie figure things out yet?"

"We're just getting started." Logan removed the bottle of painkillers from the cabinet, grabbed a can of soda from the fridge and left the kitchen.

"Here," he said, when he returned to the office and found Sadie standing where he'd left her. He opened the soda for her and shook out two pain tablets. "These will help with the swelling." That she didn't protest told him she felt worse than she let on. He wrapped the dish towel around the bag of peas and said, "Put this on your bruises and sit with your back against the couch to hold it in place."

"We've got work to do and—"

"You can't get anything done until I straighten the mess."

She did as he asked and sat down. "Thank you for the drink. I was feeling a little light-headed."

"How did Tommy fall?"

"He wanted to show me how fast he could slide across the floor in his sock feet. I was halfway up the stairs when his brakes went out and he flew off the landing."

Logan pretended to sort through the box of files sitting on the floor in front of the window while he studied Sadie's reflection in the glass. She looked tired. Raising twins on her own was no walk in the park.

"I hurt my mother once, too," he said. The comment had just slipped out. Or maybe it hadn't. Usually he avoided talking about himself, but there was something soft and comforting in Sadie's eyes, assuring him he could trust her, which was surprising, since they knew so little about each other.

"What happened?" she asked.

"I was always pestering my brothers." Out of sheer boredom. When Gunner and Reid were content to watch TV or build model sets in their bedrooms, Logan would join them, but ten minutes into the activity he'd grow bored and try to distract them. "One afternoon when we got off the school bus, I took the leftover apple from my lunch and pegged Reid in the back of the head with it."

She smiled. "I bet that hurt."

"Reid found a stone and threw it at me. Then Gunner joined in and all three of us chased one another up the driveway." Logan turned away from the window. "Reid's got a hell of an arm. He played on the baseball team in high school, but even as a ten-year-old he could throw a ball almost fifty yards."

"I hope you were a good runner."

"That day I was. I raced to the house, intent on making it to my bedroom and locking the door before my brothers caught up with me."

He shoved his fingers in his hair. "When I ran through the kitchen, I looked over my shoulder to see how close Reid was and slammed into my mother. She was frying bacon and the pan flipped over, splattering hot grease across both her arms. She ended up with second-degree burns."

"Accidents happen," Sadie said.

"It was rough seeing my mother's arms bandaged from her wrist up to her elbow."

"I'm sure she forgave you."

"I hope she did."

"Didn't she tell you that she forgave you?"

"Two months later she packed her bags and left my father."

Before his mother had taken off, he'd overheard her tell his grandparents that raising boys was difficult enough without one of them trying to kill her. Logan had felt his heart being ripped out of his chest that day. As an adult looking back on that incident, he wanted to believe his mother had spoken out of anger and frustration. But he didn't think so because that was the last time he'd seen her.

"I'm sorry."

He appreciated Sadie's sympathy. His gaze traveled around the room, trying to see the mess from her viewpoint. She must think he was totally inept. "Where do we start?"

"I'd like to examine the bank statements calling in the loan."

Logan shuffled the papers on the desk. He usually put the important stuff in the tray, but it was covered with ranch-supply catalogs. When he moved them aside, the statements were missing. He opened the file drawers—both were as messy as the top of the desk.

"Let's begin by sorting like documents into piles." Obviously Sadie assumed correctly that he was overwhelmed. "Once the desk is cleared off," she said, "we'll have space to work."

When she scooted forward on the couch, Logan held up a hand. "Stay put. Tell me how you want these papers sorted."

"Correspondence, bills and statements from the bank go together. Receipts, household bills and credit card statements in a separate pile."

"Anything else?"

"What business program do you run on the computer?" she asked.

"Business program?"

"QuickBooks? Microsoft Office?"

He clenched his teeth. "There aren't any programs on the computer." At least none that he knew of.

"That's fine. We'll do this the old-fashioned way."

It wasn't fine—they both knew his bookkeeping skills sucked.

"Can you find a few empty boxes to put the papers and documents in?" Before he answered, she added, "I'll need a notepad and a calculator or adding machine."

That sounded like a task he could handle. He went out to the hallway and lowered the trapdoor in the ceiling. The attic was stifling hot, the space cluttered with old furniture, his grandmother's hope chest and discarded toys. He opened the lid on a plastic storage bin and discovered a collection of picture books. He pulled out *Rumble in the Jungle*—Gramps's favorite book to read to Logan and his brothers—and flipped through the pages. Setting it aside, he glanced through *The Very Busy Spider*, and his thoughts drifted to the afternoon he and his brothers had trapped spiders under the back porch. Once everyone had gone to bed, he'd sneaked downstairs and let the spiders loose so they could spin a web large enough to trap Gramps when he walked through the kitchen doorway. The next morning Logan heard his grandmother screech when she discovered the kitchen crawling with spiders.

"Logan?" Sadie's voice drifted through the opening into the attic. "Did you find any boxes?"

Crap. He was supposed to be fetching boxes, not reading children's books and reminiscing about his childhood. "I'll be right down." *Focus, idiot, focus.* He turned over two boxes and a plastic milk crate, dumping their contents onto the floor. He dropped the boxes through the opening, then put a handful of books inside the crate for Tyler and carried it down the stairs before closing up the attic.

He paused in the office doorway. Sadie sat at the desk, biting her lower lip as she riffled through the mounds of papers in front of her. The afternoon sunlight spilled through the window, casting a halo of light around her blond head. If he didn't know better, he'd believe she was an angel sent to save him from himself.

She stood up and smiled. "My back feels much better. Thank you for the pain meds."

At least he'd done one thing to help Sadie. "Will these work?" He stepped farther into the room.

"Those are fine, thanks."

He set the boxes on the carpet in front of the desk. "What would you like me to do next?"

She scooped up a handful of documents. "Look through these. If you find any bank statements, put them in one of the boxes."

Logan took the pile and sat on the couch. He picked up the first paper—a credit card application—and tossed it aside. The next paper was a public auction flyer Gramps must have taken from the wall outside the Stampede Café, where people posted notices. He set it aside, then picked it up again. Why was Everett Evans selling half his herd? He should stop by the auction next weekend and find out what was happening with the man's ranch. He folded the paper and slid it into his back pocket, then walked over to the window. "Is it too sunny in here for you?"

"What?" Sadie's attention was glued to the papers in front of her.

Logan flipped the blinds, blocking the sun out, then returned to the couch and picked through the pile until he found an envelope from the bank. *Bingo!*

He started to tear the flap open, then remembered his grandfather had a letter opener. He went to the bookcase and moved things aside, positive he'd set the opener on one of the shelves after he'd used it the last time. He came up empty-handed, so he returned to the couch and read a notice about unpaid interest compounding. It looked important, so he dropped it into the box.

His phone beeped with a text message. Gunner said he'd run into a former rodeo buddy of Logan's at the Valero when he'd gassed up a few minutes ago. Logan slid the phone back into his pants pocket. He heard a noise outside in the hall and stood. "I better check to make sure I shut the attic door."

"Logan?"

He stopped and turned. Sadie's attention remained on the paper in her hand. "I can handle this," she said.

"I told you I'd help." And he'd meant it. But first he had to make sure the boys weren't getting into trouble.

"I appreciate the offer—" She looked up and the truth was plain as day in her eyes. He wasn't helping her—he was distracting her. "I'd feel better knowing you were watching the twins with your grandfather while I work."

She was letting him off the hook. He motioned to the box on the floor. "You want me to bring that over to the desk?"

"Leave it there." She smiled. "I won't need it for a while."

"I can come back and help after I see what the boys are up to."

"This could take a few hours and I don't want Tyler and Tommy to wear Emmett out."

He wasn't going to argue with her. "Gramps gets tired in the afternoons. I'll keep the boys busy." He walked over to her and removed the pen from her fingers, then scribbled his cell number on the back of the document. He doubted she'd put his number in her phone after she'd found the sticky note on the motel door yesterday morning. "In case I'm outside with the boys and you have any questions."

"Thanks."

"You want the door shut?" he asked.

"Sure, that's fine."

As soon as he closed the office door, he swallowed a curse. Just once he'd like to be able to focus long enough to make a positive impression on someone. *Sadie isn't just someone.*

She was a woman he found incredibly attractive and wanted to spend time with, preferably doing something more exciting than clerical work. But unless he got his act together, he doubted she'd give him a second look.

"Are the boys still on the back porch?" Logan asked his grandfather when he entered the kitchen.

"Got 'em shellin' peas now."

Logan walked over to the door and peered through the screen. Tyler sat on the top step, carefully opening the pods and then dumping the peas into the plastic bowl next to him. Tommy was nowhere in sight.

"Where's your brother, Tyler?" Logan stepped onto the porch.

"I don't know." Tyler kept his head down, his attention focused on his chore.

"Stay here while I look for him." Logan cut across

the yard and headed to the barn. The wheelbarrow sat outside the door where he'd left it this morning. Sweet Pea, Alamo and Mr. Biggs were in the corral eating hay. All was quiet when he entered the structure. Maybe the kid had fallen asleep in the hayloft. He climbed the ladder and checked—empty. He opened the stalls and the supply room door—no Tommy.

His heart pounded harder. The boy couldn't have gone far. He left the barn, his gaze scanning the yard and beyond. Nothing. He walked along the side of the house, but there was no sign of him.

Now Logan was worried. He returned to the kitchen. "I can't find Tommy."

"He was out there a minute ago. He can't have gone far," Gramps said.

Logan heard a clunking sound coming from beneath the porch. He nudged Gramps and pointed at their boots.

"Looks like the young'un ran off," Gramps said, stepping outside. Logan followed him.

"You like chocolate pudding, Tyler?" Gramps asked.

The boy nodded.

"Good. Since your brother's not here, you can have his bowl."

"I'm here!" a muffled voice echoed from beneath the porch.

"Did you say something, Tyler?" Gramps wiggled a finger in his ear. "I'm hearing things."

"It's me, Tommy, not Tyler." The boy popped into view. He was covered with dirt, and cobwebs stuck to his hair.

If the kid was crawling around on his hands and

knees and squeezing through a two-foot hole in the latticework, he must not be too sore from his fall down the stairs at Amelia's house.

"You're not allowed in my kitchen until you get all that dirt off of you." Gramps returned inside.

Tommy brushed off his pants, then looked at Logan. "Am I clean now?"

"Not by a long shot, kid." Logan opened the back door. "Don't move." He grabbed a towel and washcloth from the laundry room, then filled a bucket with warm water and a squirt of dish soap before returning outside.

When Tommy saw the bucket, he took a step back. "What's that for?"

Logan sat down next to Tyler and dipped the rag into the water, then handed it to Tommy. "Always wash your face first."

The boy rubbed his cheeks, then looked at Logan.

"Now your forehead," Logan said, aware Tyler had stopped shelling peas to watch his brother.

"Your neck." When Tommy finished, Logan rinsed the rag and handed it back. "Wash your hands and between your fingers."

Tommy did as he was instructed.

Logan rinsed the rag again. "Hair." After Tommy finished, he said, "Shake your head in case you have spiders hiding in your hair."

Tommy danced in a circle, and when Tyler giggled, Logan asked, "Does your brother always act this crazy?"

Tyler nodded.

"That's enough," Logan said.

Tommy staggered a few steps to the right, then

the left, until his dizziness waned. "Come here and I'll wipe off your clothes." The boy stood still while Logan ran the damp cloth over his jeans, T-shirt and the tops of his tennis shoes. "Lift up your shirt." He examined the boy's arms, chest and back for insect bites. "You got any spiders in your pants?" Tommy shook his head. "Don't go under the porch again."

"Why not?"

"There are dangerous spiders in Texas and you don't want to get near them." A bite from a brown recluse or a black widow would require a trip to the emergency room. Even though Logan sprayed the house, yard and barn every two months with a pesticide, he didn't want to take any chances with the twins' safety.

"It's your turn to shell peas for Gramps," Logan said. "Tyler's been working hard, and he deserves a break."

Tommy climbed the porch steps and took the bowl of peas from his brother.

"Get busy," Logan said. "Gramps gets grumpy when supper's late."

"Are we gonna eat here?" Tommy asked.

"I believe so." His grandfather didn't cook much anymore. The fact that he was tearing up the kitchen meant he wouldn't take no for an answer when he invited Sadie and her sons for dinner.

"Wait here, Tyler." Logan went into the house and retrieved the books he'd found in the attic. When he came back to the kitchen, he told Gramps, "Keep an eye on Tommy. I'll be in the barn with Tyler."

"Follow me, Tyler." Logan walked across the grass.

"Can I come?" Tommy called out.

"Finish shelling the peas, then you can join us." Logan glanced over his shoulder and grinned. Tommy's head was bent over the bowl, his hands furiously opening pea pods.

"What are we gonna do in the barn?" Tyler asked, his short legs pumping to keep up.

"I thought you might want to read in the hayloft again." They stopped at the ladder. "Would you like to read these?"

Tyler picked one from the pile, examined the cover and then nodded. "You climb up first. I'll follow." Once the boy was safely in the loft, Logan turned on the light and set the other books on the floor. "I need to clean Mr. Biggs's stall. Will the noise bother you?"

Tyler shook his head, then made a place for himself to sit between two bales of hay. Logan left him in peace, then climbed down the ladder and went to work. By the time he'd replaced the soiled hay in the stall with a fresh layer, a half hour had passed. He went to the doorway to check on Tommy—the boy was still on the porch shelling peas.

"Be back in a minute, Tyler." He didn't expect an answer. He'd asked the kid twice if he was okay and hadn't heard a peep out of him. The third time he'd climbed the ladder and found Tyler lying on his stomach with a book open in front of him. When the boy was reading, he blocked out the rest of the world.

Logan stopped in front of the porch. "You've been working hard."

"Am I done now?"

"Take the bowl in to Gramps and ask if that's enough peas for supper."

Tommy went inside, then returned with a big smile.

"Gramps says I did a good job. Can I go with you to the barn?"

"How would you and your brother like to clean the stock tank?"

Tommy skipped alongside Logan. "What's a stock tank?"

He pointed to the metal reservoir inside the corral. "Horses drink water out of it."

"How come you gotta clean it?"

"We need to get the algae out."

"What's algae?"

"Have you ever seen green slime?"

The boy nodded. "Anthony's mom made green slime for his birthday party and we got to take some home, but Mom threw it out 'cause it got cat hair on it."

"How did cat hair get on your slime?"

"I made a slime hat for Mr. Lucky's head."

"Who's Mr. Lucky?"

"He lives with Ms. Melanie."

"Who's… Never mind." As much as the kid's questions exasperated Logan, he got a kick out of the little guy. Sadie's ex was an idiot for not wanting to be more involved in his sons' lives. It was obvious that the twins were starving for male attention, and since their mother was helping him and Gramps, the least Logan could do was show the boys a good time.

Chapter Six

"I don't understand it." Emmett stood next to Sadie on the back porch, scratching his head. "Logan got Tommy all cleaned up after he was caught digging under the porch and now the boys are out there getting dirty all over again." With a disgusted snort he opened the screen door and muttered, "Supper's in thirty minutes."

Sadie waited until the door closed behind Emmett before she allowed herself a smile. She descended the steps, barely noticing the twinge in her back when her ears were tuned to Tyler's happy squeals. The last time she'd heard him belly laugh was when his aunt Scarlett had coaxed him into playing the tickle game. Tommy, no matter how much trouble he got into, always rolled with the punches and moved on. Whenever she was grumpy or depressed she could count on Tommy to make her smile.

She stopped in the middle of the yard and used her iPhone to snap a few pictures of the boys' laughing faces. Then she turned the camera on Logan. His T-shirt was soaked, the cotton material sticking to his muscled chest. Since her love life was nonexistent at the moment, what could it hurt to fantasize about the cowboy after she crawled into bed at night?

She slipped the phone into her pocket and watched as Logan lifted her shirtless sons by the backs of their pants, twirled them in a slow circle, then plopped them into the three-foot metal pool. The boys popped to the surface, and Logan fished them out of the water and set them on their bare feet.

"Do it again, Uncle Logan!" Tommy yelled.

"Please!" Tyler pleaded.

Logan tossed them into the tank, and this time when the boys surfaced they dodged his hands and instead splashed each other. Sadie couldn't recall the last time her sons had roughhoused together. Tyler usually avoided wrestling with his brother because Tommy became too wild. When she'd asked the pediatrician about putting Tommy on medication, the pills he'd prescribed had caused insomnia, so they'd taken him off the meds.

Sadie had then visited her local library and checked out every book she could find on ADD. She'd tried implementing several parenting techniques—some had worked, others hadn't. But it wasn't until she'd begun establishing a routine and sticking with it, even on the weekends, that she'd noticed an improvement in their home life. When Tommy created havoc, she tried to maintain a positive attitude and keep her frustration in check, which helped Tyler stay calm, too, and eased some of the tension between her sons.

Logan lifted the boys out of the water and Tommy shook his head, spraying him in the face. Tyler copied his brother, laughing when Logan made a big production of being outraged. His boisterous chuckle reminded Sadie of how lonely she'd been the past couple of years. Her experience with Pete hadn't soured her on marriage. She still yearned to find a man she could share her life with. A man who would be a father to the twins not because they were part of a package deal, but because he cared about them and *wanted* to be their father.

If she'd watched this scene before she'd witnessed Logan's inability to focus in the office, she'd be tempted to see where her attraction to him led. But she'd done enough research on ADD to recognize the signs in Logan. She couldn't imagine having both a child and a husband with ADD. She'd go crazy if these spur-of-the-moment activities happened every day of their lives. There was no way to determine if Tommy's ADD would become worse or better as he grew older, but regardless, he needed two organized, efficient parents to keep him on track. If his parents weren't on the same page all the time, Tommy's day-to-day life could become overwhelming.

Logan dumped the boys into the tank again before tossing a soccer ball to them. The three played catch, the twins bouncing on their toes. All the swim lessons she'd paid for were coming in handy because the boys had no trouble keeping afloat in water that was up to their necks. She hated to end the fun, but fifteen minutes had passed since Emmett had announced dinner in a half hour. She returned to the house. "Emmett, do you have any old towels the boys can dry off with?"

"In there." He pointed over his shoulder.

She entered the laundry room, her eyes widening at the mess. Three baskets sat on the floor, overflowing with clothes, and the ironing board was buried under a pile of Western shirts. She rummaged through the cupboards and found the towels.

"Do you need help setting the table?" she asked as she passed through the kitchen.

"The boys can do it when they come inside."

Sadie left the house, and when Logan spotted her coming, he waved. "I didn't know you were having a pool party." She stopped at his side.

"I can toss you in, too, if you'd like."

She laughed. "You'd throw your back out."

His gaze roamed over her, an appreciative gleam in his eyes, and her face warmed. "I could easily toss you in. Want me to prove it?"

"I'll take your word for it. Right now the little monsters need to get out of the water and dry off for supper." She handed Logan a towel. "You take one, and I'll take the other."

She thought for sure he'd reach for Tommy, but instead, he said, "Tyler, come over here." Logan lifted him out of the water and set him on the ground, then rubbed the towel over the boy's hair until it stood on end.

"That was fun," Tommy said as Sadie dried him off.

"Had I known playing in water was on the agenda today, I would have made you two wear your swim trunks."

Logan set Tyler on the corral rail. "Hold tight and I'll put your shoes on." After he helped Tyler, he hoisted Tommy onto the rail and did the same for him.

"Grandpa Emmett needs your help in the kitchen," Sadie said. "Go up to the house and do as he says."

Once the boys were out of earshot, Sadie spoke. "Thank you."

"For what?"

"For being nice to my sons. Tommy can wear you out fast."

"I can relate to him."

"I know." Sadie's mouth curved. "You have ADD, too."

He rolled a stone on the ground beneath his boot. "It's that obvious, huh?"

"Only because I have a son with ADD."

Logan rubbed the side of his nose, obviously embarrassed that she'd picked up on the disorder.

"You're very patient with the twins," she said. "They haven't been this happy in a long time." There were questions in Logan's eyes, and since they were family now that Lydia and Gunner had married, there was no reason for secrets between them. "Pete didn't help out much with the twins. The boys were a lot of work and there wasn't any sleep for either of us the first year, but I thought he'd come around."

"He left because he couldn't handle Tommy?" Logan asked.

"No, I filed for divorce because Pete cheated on me."

"I'm sorry."

She waited for him to tell her why he'd gotten divorced, but he left her hanging and she didn't know what to make of that. Had one of them cheated? Or had there been another reason for the split?

"Do the boys miss their father?" he asked.

"I don't think it's an issue of missing him as much as they don't understand why he chose to live with another woman and her children over them."

"It's always the kids who suffer when families break up."

"Was it rough when your mother left?" she asked.

Logan nodded. "After she disappeared, Dad took off for longer stretches and Gramps was stuck riding herd over us boys and taking care of the ranch. Grandma Sara had her hands full with the household chores." He grinned. "As you might expect, my brothers and I ran wild most of the time."

Wild. Logan had hit upon one of Sadie's fears when she thought of Tommy's future. She worried that if he didn't learn how to manage his ADD the right way, his behavior might take a turn for the worse and she'd be making numerous trips to the principal's office. And heaven forbid later in life, the police station.

"And what about you?" he asked.

"What about me?"

"Do you miss the boys' father?"

Sadie got lost in Logan's brown gaze and she couldn't look away if she wanted to. Had he taken a step closer or had she? Inches separated their bodies. A stiff breeze against her back would push her into Logan's arms and then... "No," she said. "I don't miss Pete."

Logan's face drew closer. This was crazy.

"I've been wanting to do this since you showed up at the motel Friday night." His breath caressed her lips a second before...the touch of his mouth sent a jolt through her body that reminded her she wasn't only a mother but also a woman with needs that had gone unfulfilled for too long.

He ended the kiss and trailed his finger down the

side of her neck before he lowered his arm. "Your ex is a fool. You're better off without him."

Her heart beat as if she were a giddy teenager with her first crush. Logan wasn't only kind to the boys, he was good for her ego. "We'd better get back to the house before Tommy breaks all the supper dishes."

When they entered the kitchen, the twins were naked except for the dish towels tied around their waists.

"What happened to your clothes?" she asked.

"I put 'em in the dryer," Emmett said. Right then the machine buzzed.

"Follow me, boys." Sadie went into the laundry room, removed their superhero underwear and jeans from the dryer, and helped them dress. Back in the kitchen she said, "What can I do?"

"Pour the critters some milk."

"What are you drinking, Emmett?" she asked.

"Water'll be fine."

She looked at Logan and he nodded. "Same for me."

Sadie removed three bottles of water and then poured milk into two glasses before sitting next to the twins. "It smells wonderful," she said.

"Shepherd's pie was one of Sara's favorites." Emmett placed the casserole on the table, then added a loaf of warm bread and the butter dish.

Logan served the boys first.

"What do you say?" Sadie stared at her sons.

"Thank you," they said in unison.

Logan handed the serving spoon to her, and after she filled the twins' plates and her own, she passed it to Emmett, who in turn gave it back to Logan.

The boys ate quietly—a first for them. Usually

Tommy talked nonstop during mealtime. The physical activity must have worn down his battery.

Emmett spoke to the twins. "Next time you two take a swim in the horse trough bring me back some of that algae and I'll put it in a salad."

"Eeew! I'm not gonna eat algae." Tommy stuck his tongue out.

"You ever eat seaweed?" Emmett asked Tyler. Her son shook his head. "Seaweed grows in the Pacific Ocean," Gramps said, "and it tastes like salty lettuce."

"Where's the ocean?" Tommy asked.

"Over there." Gramps pointed at the kitchen wall facing west.

"Uncle Logan, can we go see the ocean?" Tommy asked.

"Have you ever visited California?" Logan looked at Sadie.

"We haven't," she said, "but we've been to Florida to see my parents. The boys were only two, and we didn't spend any time at the ocean."

"We've got a creek that runs through the property," Gramps said. "You boys ever been fishing before?"

Tommy and Tyler shook their heads.

"A while back I caught a fish this big." Emmett set his fork down and then spread his arms wide. "Almost pulled me into the water."

Logan shifted in his chair, his knee bumping Sadie's thigh beneath the table. She glanced at him, but he acted as if he wasn't aware they touched, so she let her leg rest against his knee.

After several fishing stories, Emmett pushed his plate away and looked at Sadie. "You figure out yet if the bank's right and we owe them money?"

Logan stiffened as if he was bracing for a blow.

"Actually, I didn't," Sadie said. Since Logan and his brothers now held the ranch mortgage, she thought it was only right to speak with Logan first. It was up to him to share the news with Emmett. "I'm still sorting through the paperwork." She glanced at Logan. "I can return tomorrow or take the papers and documents back to my aunt's house and work there."

"No." The word burst from Logan's mouth, causing Emmett to raise an eyebrow. "You can use the office in the house as long as you need it."

"I don't mind keeping an eye on these ragamuffins." Emmett winked at the twins.

"Are you sure?" Sadie asked.

"Gramps and I will entertain them," Logan said.

He sounded sure of himself, but Sadie knew from experience that any activity with the boys could turn into a fiasco. "I don't want them to get in the way of your chores."

"They can help me," Logan said.

Emmett nodded. "I'll tag along and make sure they don't get into any trouble."

Sadie studied her sons' pleading eyes. She didn't want to be Debbie Downer, and this trip was supposed to be a fun break from their everyday routine. "I guess we could try it for a few days."

Gramps shoved his chair back. "Who wants chocolate pie?"

"You and the boys take your dessert out to the porch," Logan said. "Sadie and I will clean up." Left alone in the kitchen together, she rinsed the dishes and loaded them into the dishwasher while Logan put the food away. When he lightly touched her lower back as he reached for the plastic wrap on the counter, she closed her eyes and imagined the feel of his hands gliding over her bare skin.

"How are your bruises?" His breath hit the side of her face and a shudder ran through her.

"Better."

They worked in silence for several minutes before Logan asked, "Why'd you cover for me?"

"What do you mean?"

"You found the notices from the bank, didn't you?"

"Yes." Sadie wished with all her heart she could wave a magic wand and help Logan out of the jam he'd gotten himself into.

"We had some unexpected expenses the past few months," he said.

"I saw the bill for the new septic system." And she'd seen other receipts that weren't normal monthly bills.

He stared out the window above the sink. "I never wanted this responsibility, but someone had to step up and keep the place going when Gramps's drinking grew worse."

"Your grandfather's an alcoholic?"

"He drank on and off in spurts for years. He quit when my grandmother became ill. Then my father died and that was all it took for Gramps's drinking to get out of control again." Logan rolled his shoulders as if the memory was uncomfortable. "I told him I'd come home if he gave up the booze, and he agreed. He's been sober ever since."

Logan didn't only carry the weight of the ranch on his shoulders but the well-being of his grandfather.

"There are more fun things to do with your time

in Stampede than looking into our financial mess," he said.

"The boys are having fun. That's all that matters."

"Just say the word and I'll find a way out of this mess myself."

"Logan." She held his gaze. "I want to help you because it's been too long since I've heard Tyler laugh the way he did when you let the boys play in the water earlier. And it's been months since I've seen my sons have so much fun together." She spread her arms wide. "Being able to run around on this ranch is exactly what they need right now, and I'm grateful that you're willing to have them here."

Sadie would be lying to herself if she didn't admit that she was a little worried the boys would grow attached to Logan and his grandfather, but it was reassuring to know that the Hardell men were now part of their family and the twins would have a long-term relationship with them.

"I'd rather not take your aunt up on her offer to pay off the bank," he said. "Any chance you can come up with a way to get us out of this jam?"

"You and your brothers could sell."

Logan dropped his gaze. "Gramps wants the ranch to stay in the family. One of Gunner and Lydia's future children or Reid's will want to run it some day."

"Or maybe one of your kids." Logan's face turned ashen and his eyes glazed over. "Did I say something wrong?" She touched his arm but he backed up a step, and her hand fell away.

"I won't be having any kids of my own." He walked out of the room, leaving Sadie staring at his retreating back.

"Mom!" Tommy shouted through the screen door.

"What?"

"Can Gramps come over to Aunt Amelia's house and play with us in the attic?"

Startled by Logan's behavior, Sadie didn't immediately answer her son.

"Mom?"

She opened the screen door and joined the group on the back porch. "You'll have to ask Aunt Amelia if you can have a playdate with Gramps at her house."

"Where's Logan?" Emmett asked.

A truck engine revved to life and Sadie said, "He had an errand to run." By the time she and the boys reached the van in the front yard, the taillights of Logan's pickup were tiny specs in the distance.

"WHAT DO YOU think of Logan?" Lydia asked Monday morning. Sadie had offered to help her cousin organize the kitchen cupboards in the downtown apartment Lydia and Gunner were renovating.

"The boys love hanging around Logan and Emmett." No way was she confessing that Logan had kissed her. Or that he'd walked off after he'd told her he wasn't having any kids of his own. She still didn't know what that meant. Sadie pressed her fingertips to her mouth and closed her eyes, imagining the tingle she'd felt when his lips had touched hers. As much as Logan's attraction to her made her feel feminine and desirable, she didn't dare start anything with him. Logan wasn't the calm, organized, efficient marriage partner she was looking for to help her raise the boys. And since they were family now, it would be awkward between them when she visited her aunt and cousin in the future if they'd crossed the line with each other.

Sadie climbed onto the step stool and placed the wineglasses on the shelf. "Logan let the boys jump into the stock tank and pick out the algae."

Lydia laughed. "I didn't ask how your sons liked Logan, I asked how *you* did."

"He's a nice man." With a few secrets. "Do you know why he and his wife divorced?"

"Nope. Logan doesn't talk about it, but Gunner assumes she didn't like living on the ranch. Speaking of small-town life…"

Sadie glanced over her shoulder.

"Is Stampede a place you and the boys could see yourselves living?"

"What's with all the questions?" Sadie climbed down from the stool.

Lydia placed her hand on the gentle swell of her stomach. "Tommy and Tyler would have a little cousin to play with and you'd have more family to help with the boys if you moved here."

The twins would definitely benefit from being around more family.

Lydia released a long sigh. "I'm nervous about being a first-time mother. I could really use your support."

Sadie sat at the table and held her cousin's hand. "You will make a great mother." She smiled. "The boys and I have only been here a couple of days, but I admit that already Stampede is feeling more like home than Madison ever did."

"Then look for a job here. I'm sure you could find a position in one of the towns nearby. South San Antonio is only an hour away."

Sadie didn't doubt she could land a good-paying job with benefits in the Alamo City. But the preschool Tommy was on a waiting list to get into was highly regarded and she had to do what was best for him first. Hoping her cousin would drop the subject, Sadie said, "I'll give it some thought."

"Did you figure out the snafu with the bank?" Lydia asked.

"It'll be a while yet before I have all the numbers in order. The boys and I are heading out to the ranch again this afternoon."

"When Logan came home to take over, Gunner would offer to help with chores, but Logan always insisted he had things under control. Then whenever Gunner pointed out something that needed to be done, Logan would become defensive and they'd argue. So Gunner stayed away and only helped when Logan asked him to, which wasn't often."

Feeling protective of Logan, Sadie said, "Men have their pride."

"Since you've been around Emmett the past couple of days, has he said anything about Aunt Amelia?"

"No, why?"

"Gunner and I are positive that she's in love with Emmett. Maybe while you're here you can coax him to confide in you and find out if he feels the same way about Aunt Amelia."

"I intend to mind my own business." Sadie owed Emmett that much for helping to entertain the twins at the ranch. She moved the stool in front of a different cabinet and began putting away the plates and bowls.

"Let's plan a Labor Day picnic at the ranch," Lydia

said. "We'll get Amelia and Emmett together and see what happens."

Sadie laughed. "You are so bad." She finished stacking the dishes, then checked the time on her iPhone. "I better get going before the boys exhaust Aunt Amelia."

Lydia walked Sadie downstairs to the front door. "I love what you did with this store," Sadie said, admiring the reclaimed barn door that served as her cousin's desk.

"I landed two new clients last week. A couple in Mesquite and a Realtor in Rocky Point who wants me to decorate his office with a Western theme."

"That's great news."

"Gunner and I are fortunate that Aunt Amelia is so generous with her money. With the building paid off and no mortgage it's less scary to start a family."

"She's been good to all of us, hasn't she?" Sadie stepped onto the sidewalk. "I'll talk to you soon."

Lydia waved. "Good luck with Logan and Emmett today."

Luck? Sadie would need a better strategy than luck to help keep her guard up around Logan.

Chapter Seven

"Gramps," Logan called out when he walked through the back door Monday afternoon. "Did we get rid of that old Radio Flyer wagon Dad bought Reid when he was little?"

His grandfather stood at the sink washing a watermelon. "Think it's in the shed. Why?"

"Sadie texted me that she and the boys will be here in a few minutes. I thought the kids might like a ride in the wagon."

"I'm taking my fishing pole to the creek later. The boys can tag along with me if you want to work in the office with Sadie."

"I can't help. I've got to haul hay out to the feeders." The hay hauling could wait until tomorrow, but Logan was looking for any excuse to avoid Sadie after his embarrassing blunder last night when he'd blurted out that he wouldn't be having any children of his own. The only reason he could come up with for sharing that intimate detail was that Sadie had been sympathetic and understanding about his ADD.

"You should invite Sadie to go along with you when you check on the herd. Show her the ranch."

Logan headed for the back door.

"That gal shouldn't have to work the whole time she's out here," Gramps said.

Logan couldn't agree more. He left the porch and walked to the shed, which sat next to the storm shelter his father had dug in the backyard when Logan and his brothers were little. They'd taken cover in the bunker a handful of times over the years, but it had mostly been used to store their grandmother's canned fruits and vegetables.

The shed was filled with junk and Logan had to move things around to get to the wagon. He smiled when he saw the huge dent on the side of the Radio Flyer. When his brothers were in elementary school, they'd piled into the wagon and ridden it down a wooden ramp their grandfather had constructed. They'd lost control and had crashed into the side of their father's pickup. Logan had been riding in the front and had walked away with a knot on his forehead the size of an egg. Gunner and Reid had bailed out seconds before impact.

He carried the wagon to the spigot and hosed it off, making sure no spiders hid in the wheels, then he left it to dry in the sun. He'd almost made it to the pickup when the white minivan turned into the driveway. Now what? If he took off without waiting to say hello, Sadie would guess he was avoiding her. Playing it cool was his only option.

The front door opened and his grandfather stepped outside. The old man had been up at the crack of dawn doing laundry and making pudding pops for the boys. He hadn't shown this much enthusiasm for domestic chores in a long time.

"Gramps!" Tommy yelled as soon as the van door

opened. He climbed out of his booster seat. "What are we gonna do today?" The kid charged up the steps, skidded to a stop and then turned around. "Hi, Uncle Logan."

"How goes it, Tommy?" Logan smiled at the boy. Tyler walked toward him carrying his backpack of books. "How are you, Tyler?" The boy peeked up at him and offered a shy smile.

"You kids want to go fishing?" Gramps asked.

"Can we, Mom?" the boys asked Sadie.

She stopped next to the bushes, her gaze swinging between Logan and his grandfather. "How deep is the creek, Emmett?"

"Might be over their heads in the middle. They can wear life jackets if you want."

"If you agree to wear a life jacket, you can go fishing with Gramps," she told the boys.

"Did you hear that, Gramps?" Tommy said. "We can fish."

"I heard." Gramps descended the porch steps. "The jackets are in the shed."

"No wandering off by yourself," Sadie said. "Did you hear me, Tommy?"

"They won't wander," Gramps said, "unless they want to wrestle a bear."

Tyler's eyes widened. "What bear?"

"Follow me and I'll tell you all about Bruiser." Tommy reached for Gramps's hand and Tyler trailed the pair.

"Bruiser's as big as the state of Texas. Came through here about ten years ago." The rest of Emmett's tall tale was lost when they turned the corner of the house, leaving Logan and Sadie alone.

"It's a shame to have to work inside on such a beautiful day," she said.

The knot in Logan's stomach unraveled. If she could act like nothing weird had happened between them yesterday, then so could he. "Before you get started in the office, how about a tour of the ranch? I need to drop off a couple of hay bales at the feeder, and then we can stop at the creek and check on the boys."

"I'd love that."

"Gramps made iced tea this morning if you want to have a glass while I put the bales onto the flatbed."

"Thanks." She inched past him and he caught a hint of her flowery perfume. Before he did something stupid like turn around and follow her into the house, he made a beeline to the barn, conscious of the extra bounce in his step.

OH, MY... WOW.

The sip of iced tea detoured into Sadie's lungs as she stood at the kitchen window, watching Logan whisk his T-shirt off and hang it over the corral rail. He hopped into his truck and backed it up to the trailer, then got out and hitched the flatbed, his muscles bunching. Next he disappeared into the barn, and a minute later the loft door opened and a bale of hay fell onto the flatbed. When it stopped raining bales, she helped herself to two bottles of water from the fridge and went outside. "Thirsty?" she asked when Logan stepped from the barn.

"Thanks." He wiped his forearm across his sweaty brow before drinking half the bottle of water. "It's hotter than I thought."

Logan's comment went over Sadie's head as she

stared at his naked chest, mesmerized by a bead of sweat that rolled between his pectoral muscles and then bounced over his washboard abs before coming to a stop inside his belly button.

"Sadie?"

Her gaze flew to his face. His brown eyes sparkled with humor. Caught in the act, there was no sense pretending she didn't find him attractive. "You have a nice chest."

His grin widened. "I'd return the compliment, but that might be pushing it."

If one of them didn't change the subject, the tour of the ranch would become a tour of Logan's bedroom.

"Hop in the truck," he said, "and turn on the air conditioner while I slide the bales into place."

Grateful to put some space between them, she did as he suggested and then directed the air vents at her heated face. After Logan finished arranging the bales, he rinsed off with the hose, patted his chest dry with a towel and slipped his T-shirt back on. A minute later they traveled down a dirt road, heading straight for the horizon.

"This life is so different from mine." She gestured at the pastureland whizzing by the truck. "When I drive to work, I see cars, school buses and stoplights. You see wide-open spaces, barbed wire, scrubland and prairie coneflowers."

He glanced at her. "Sometimes I have to brake for jackrabbits."

She laughed. "How many cattle do you have on the property?"

"We try to keep around a hundred and twenty-five head."

"Do you hire help when calving season starts?"

"We don't have bulls on the ranch anymore. We buy our heifers and steers at auction and raise them until they're big enough to sell to feedlots." He slowed the truck before he drove over a bump in the road. "Gramps quit messing with calving season a long time ago. It was too hard for him to herd cows and grandkids."

"Do you grow your own hay?"

"We used to but now we buy hay from a supplier north of town."

Sadie stared out the window, noticing the occasional cluster of river oaks, thinking the shade beneath the trees would be the perfect place for a picnic. "I don't see any cows."

"They're a ways out here. We rotate the animals between three pastures. We've got two wells on the property that draw water from the creek, which is over that way." He pointed in the direction opposite to the one they were traveling.

"I think I see cows up ahead." She leaned forward, the seat belt cutting into her.

"They wait by the feeder." He took his foot off the accelerator and coasted up to the square container made of large metal pipes with enough space between them for the cows to stick their heads through and eat the hay.

"Stay in the pickup." He nodded to her sandals. "I'd hate for a cow to step on those pretty toes." Logan got out and jumped onto the flatbed. The bovines bellowed, their tails swishing.

Sadie lowered her window and breathed in nature—hay, animals and dust.

After Logan finished throwing the bales into the feeder, he got into the pickup and she asked, "What's that land formation over there?" The rocky ridge sat higher in elevation than the rest of the ranch.

"That's the area your aunt wants to have the trail rides. I'll show you." As they drove closer, Sadie saw wildflowers growing between the crevices in the rocky terrain.

"Where would the trail go?" she asked, after he parked and they got out.

He pointed east, where the ground sloped downward. "The trail would most likely start over there and then head north, curving around the back side of the ridge before ending up on the west side where we are now." He motioned to the area a few yards away. "A barn and corral would have to be built over there for the horses."

"If you followed the route you mentioned," she said, "how long would the trail ride last?"

"Maybe an hour."

"What about running water?" she asked.

"We'd have to dig another well."

She shielded her eyes from the sun and glanced around. "Where would you suggest putting the petting zoo?"

"Small animals need to be closer to the house. They'd be too vulnerable out here by themselves."

"So the best place would be on the other side of the ranch?"

Logan nodded.

"It makes sense. If the zoo was near the house, your grandfather could keep an eye on the animals."

Logan's lips flattened as he stared into space. "There's no chance the bank made a mistake?"

"No, but I still haven't sorted through all of the statements."

Sadie thought back to her first real fight with Peter when she was nine months pregnant. Both of their paychecks had been automatically deposited in the bank and it had been Pete's job to pay the bills. Then one afternoon she'd opened the mail and discovered an eviction notice because their rent hadn't been paid in two months. When she checked their account and saw the low balance, she'd questioned Pete. He'd confessed that he'd spent their money on another woman. His affair had forced them to find a new place to live and their credit rating had taken a huge hit. He'd asked Sadie for a second chance and for the sake of the twins she'd given him one, but she'd never trusted him again with their money and had taken over the finances.

As much as Sadie enjoyed Logan's company and found him sexy, she'd be wise not to indulge in that attraction. She had enough problems of her own to manage, and a man who didn't have his act together would only add more stress to her life.

"I'm sure it's not easy keeping up with the ranch all by yourself."

"Don't make excuses for me, Sadie. I screwed up." He walked a few feet and stabbed the toe of his boot in the dirt. "The truth is, I've always had trouble focusing. I can't even read the electric bill without thinking of fifty other things I should be doing instead." He faced her. "Maybe I can find a way out of this mess."

"I doubt the bank will approve another loan."

"The office is a mess. Maybe you missed something."

Logan's pleading gaze squeezed Sadie's heart. "It's possible. I'm still going through all the statements," she said.

"Take as much time as you need."

"I'll have to bring the boys with me, and I'm not sure your grandfather's up to babysitting them every day."

"I'll help out with Tommy and Tyler."

"I can also set up a filing system for you in the office and download a software program on your computer that will help you keep track of future expenses and receipts. And I'd be happy to teach you how to use it."

"Deal." He took her hand and led her back to the pickup.

WHEN LOGAN PULLED up to the creek and parked, Sadie didn't see the trio anywhere. "Where are they?"

"Probably downstream. We'll have to hike there." His gaze dropped to her sandals. "Can you walk on the uneven ground in those things?"

"I'll manage." She unsnapped her seat belt, then followed Logan along the dirt path parallel to the water, which was the width of a traffic lane on the highway.

"There they are." Logan pointed ahead of them.

Emmett slouched in his lawn chair next to the water. Tyler sat with his back against a tree, his head buried in a book, still wearing his life jacket. Tommy squatted at the edge of the stream, poking around in the mud with a stick.

"Heads up, you've got company!" Logan called when they were a few feet away.

"Mom!" Tommy sprinted toward her, his life jacket bouncing up and down, smacking his chin.

"Catch any fish?" she asked.

He shook his head. "Fishing's boring."

Sadie sniffed. "It certainly smells stinky around here."

"We haven't had rain in a while," Emmett said. "We need a gully washer to get the water moving again." He handed the pole to Logan, who walked downstream and recast the line.

Tommy went back to jabbing his stick into the mud.

"This spot is peaceful," Sadie said.

"Sara used to come out here to get away from the boys when they were tearing up the house."

"Look, Gramps." Tommy held up a rock. "It's gold!" He raced over and held out his treasure.

Emmett made a big production of examining the stone. "I think you may have found the mother lode."

"What's a mother lode?" Tommy looked at Sadie, but Logan answered.

"It means you'll be rich."

"I'm gonna be rich." Tommy stuffed the rock into the pocket of his shorts.

"Whatcha gonna do with all your money?" Emmett asked.

"Give it to my mom so she doesn't cry when my dad forgets to pay our preschool."

Sadie wanted to find a hole and crawl into it. Tommy made it sound like she was a basket case when in fact he'd seen her cry only once since the divorce—

but obviously once had been enough to leave a lasting memory.

Emmett stretched his arms over his head. "I've been sitting too long." He looked at Sadie. "You want to walk farther up the trail and see Sara's wild daisies?"

"I'd love to."

"Don't let these rascals out of your sight, Logan," Emmett said.

Sadie caught the worried look in Logan's eyes before she turned away. Was he concerned his grandfather might ask questions about the ranch's financial situation?

Sadie followed the older man along the path and as soon as they were out of hearing range of Logan and the boys, he asked, "How soon before you know where the ranch stands with the bank?"

"Soon." She glanced at the cloudless sky and attempted to distract Emmett. "I should be working right now, but it's such a nice day."

Emmett pointed ahead on the trail to an explosion of black-eyed Susans. "I'd bring a rocking chair out here after one of Sara's chemo treatments and she'd sit with her flowers, soaking up the sun." He knelt down and brushed an inch of dust off a decorative stone partially hidden by the daisies. Sadie peered over Emmett's shoulder. The image of an angel with wings had been engraved on the rock, along with the names Sara and Donald.

"We spread her and Donny's ashes here."

"It's a beautiful resting spot, Emmett."

"Amelia suggested it. Glad she did."

After seeing the sacred garden and learning her aunt had played a role in picking her best friend's final resting place, Sadie knew without a doubt that Amelia would never allow the bank to take the ranch, regardless of whether or not Emmett agreed to participate in her plans for a tourist attraction on his property. If Sadie didn't know better, she'd think her aunt's interference in Emmett's business was not only an attempt to force him to engage in life more but also to get him to notice her and see her not as his adversary, but as a woman who genuinely cared about him.

"I was leafing through a flower book in the office and saw Sara's handwritten notes in the margins."

"She was always wanting to plant something. The rosebushes in front of the house used to bloom most of the year. Once Sara got a look at Amelia's crepe myrtle trees, she had to have some for our driveway." Emmett rubbed his hands together. "After she was gone, I didn't have the energy to fuss with the bushes or keep her garden going."

"There's a garden?"

"Along the side of the house. It's overgrown with weeds now."

"Back in Madison I was on the landscape committee at our apartment complex. It's been my experience that with a little TLC, most rosebushes can be brought back to life."

"Sara and Amelia used to go to the garden center in Rocky Point every Saturday to check out the sales." Emmett eyed Sadie. "What's your aunt up to today?"

"She said something about driving into Rocky Point later today to check out an art exhibit with a friend."

"That woman runs around like a twenty-year-old. If she doesn't slow down, she's liable to wake up dead one morning."

Sadie laughed. "Aunt Amelia is happiest when she's busy."

"Busy in everybody's business." He cleared his throat. "When are you and the boys heading back to Wisconsin?"

"Not anytime soon. I don't have to worry about finding a job right away and the twins are enjoying a break from preschool, so we'll be sticking around."

Emmett nodded as if the news pleased him. "We've got plenty to do here to keep 'em occupied while you're in the office."

"I appreciate you supervising them, but we don't want to wear out our welcome."

Emmett glanced sideways at Sadie. "Logan was a lot like Tommy when he was little. Always on the go."

Always on the go was a nice way of saying a kid was hyperactive.

"Logan's mother couldn't handle him," he said. "And Donny was never around to keep him in line. I put Logan to work, hoping to tire him out. I should have been fairer about divvying up the chores between my grandsons, but I made Logan work harder so he'd get into less trouble."

"I've tried chores with the boys, but Tommy always loses interest after and Tyler's the one who picks up the slack."

"Tyler's a good helper in the kitchen," Emmett said. "He likes to measure ingredients."

"I was talking to Lydia and we thought it might be nice to have a Labor Day picnic at the ranch. We could have it on Sunday unless you have other plans."

"My only plan each day is to open my eyes in morning to see if I'm still breathing."

Sadie smiled. "That shepherd's pie was tasty the other night. What do you suggest for the picnic?"

Emmett's eyes lit up. "I can fry up a chicken."

"Lydia and I will make the salads."

"Put together a grocery list and I'll drive into Mesquite and buy what we need. I don't mind doing all the cooking. Tyler can help me."

"I'll tell Aunt Amelia to bring the dessert, then."

"You might remind her that I'm partial to apple pie," he said, then pointed to the trail. "We'd best get back to the boys."

As Sadie followed Emmett along the creek, she made a silent vow to Sara that she'd try to save her rosebushes.

Chapter Eight

Wednesday evening Logan rapped his knuckles against the office door.

"Come in."

When he stepped into the room, Sadie offered a tired smile that didn't reach her eyes and his gut clenched with guilt. She didn't have to help him, but out of the goodness of her heart—and because she appreciated the time he was spending with her sons— she was examining hundreds of legal papers, receipts and invoices. He thought back to his childhood and had no memory of his mother making any kind of sacrifices for him.

"Are the boys behaving?" She set down her pen and leaned back in the chair. "I haven't heard a peep out of them since supper two hours ago."

"They're sitting on the couch with Gramps, watching reruns of *Hee-Haw*. Actually, I think Tommy's watching and Tyler's reading a book." He walked across the rug and stopped in front of the window. "It's getting darker earlier in the evenings."

"You can tell already?"

He turned, forcing himself to face the desk—the symbol of his failure. He wanted to spend time away from the office with Sadie, but she'd never get anything done if he kept interrupting her.

"Did you know your grandfather took out a second mortgage on the property before your grandmother passed away?"

He didn't know, but things were becoming clearer. Logan sank onto the couch and closed his eyes. "Gramps probably needed the money to pay medical bills. He drove Grandma Sara to some famous cancer doctor in Houston. They'd stay for days at a time while she received radiation and chemo treatments."

"That explains the hotel receipts from way back then," she said.

"The treatments bought my grandmother an extra year, that's it." He stood and paced in front of the desk. "It makes sense now why Gramps had to borrow money from Amelia to buy the Moonlight Motel for my grandmother."

"He bought the motel for Sara?"

"Grandma always wished someone would buy the property and restore the place." Logan picked up the paperweight on the corner of the desk. He rolled the colored glass ball between his hands. "When it became clear that she was losing the battle with her health, Gramps bought the motel, hoping it would lift her spirits and give her the will to keep fighting." He set the weight down and walked back to the window. The side of the house faced east, and long gray shadows were creeping across the property.

"I didn't know the motel was special to your grandmother. I bet she'd be happy to see how nice the renovations turned out."

Logan drew in a deep breath, then nodded at the

piles of paperwork in front of Sadie. "It's obvious I dropped the ball and I should have kept better track of the finances."

"You've got a lot on your shoulders."

"I appreciate you making excuses for me, but if I don't get my act together, we could lose Paradise Ranch." When Sadie looked away, Logan's stomach bottomed out.

"There's no way for me to get out from under this debt without having to accept your aunt's money, is there?"

She shook her head.

"What about selling off some of our assets?"

"I could look into that," she said.

"If there are no other options, then I'll persuade Gramps to get on board with Amelia's idea." He was putting Sadie in a tight spot, asking her to work in his best interests and not her aunt's. "Do we have much time before the bank makes a move?"

"Not really." She nibbled her lower lip.

"I'm willing to watch the boys every day for however long it takes you to wade through the papers."

"What about your own chores?" she asked.

"The boys can help me with the horses and Gramps will keep an eye on them when I'm checking the cattle." He nodded to the desk. "Tell me what to look for and I'll go through the documents after you leave tonight." He'd stay up until dawn to help Sadie, in the hope that she could wave a magic wand and make all of Logan's problems vanish.

She stared him in the eye and he sensed she had her doubts that he would follow through. Anxiety clawed its way into his throat. If he didn't know better, he'd think he'd climbed the chute rails and had settled on the back of a rank bull. Just when he expected her to say no, she said, "Okay."

The blood rushed from his head and he leaned against the bookcase.

"After the boys and I leave tonight, I want you to sort through the box on the floor by the couch. Collect all the receipts, no matter how old."

"Done." The task didn't sound difficult. "And like I said earlier, I'd like to take you up on your offer to teach me how to use a business software program." He didn't want her believing that all her work would be for nothing.

"I've already set up a business program on your computer. I'd be happy to show you how to use it."

"And there's something else," he said.

"What's that?"

"I was hoping you'd call it quits for the night and take a walk with me before it gets too dark."

Her smile took the edge off his anxiety. "A walk sounds nice." She followed him from the room, down the hallway and out the back door. "Where are we going?"

"You'll see." He grasped her hand and they cut across the yard, disappearing into the woods at the back of the property.

"The trees are huge," she said.

"My great-grandfather planted them as soon as he bought the land."

"Wait." She tugged her hand free and pointed several yards away. "Is that your grandmother's garden?"

"Grandma Sara grew her own vegetables."

Sadie looked longingly at the plot of land over-grown with weeds.

"Grandma would plant pumpkins in the fall, and my brothers and I had fun destroying them after Hal-loween."

"Destroying them?"

"We'd climb into the hayloft and toss them out the door to watch them splatter on the ground. Then we'd feed the pieces to the horses." He led her behind the trees and along a narrow path.

"What's back here?" she asked.

"You'll see." A short distance later he stopped in front of a grassy mound about four feet high. "This was my hiding place when I got into trouble."

"There's an opening."

"I dug a cave," he said.

Sadie got on her knees and peered inside the open-ing. "It's not very big."

"Plenty big enough for a little boy." He climbed on top of the hill and reclined. Sadie joined him. "I'd grab the flashlight and come out here after Gramps had fallen asleep in front of the TV. I did a lot of star-gazing and dreaming about being anywhere but on the ranch."

"Tell me."

He rolled his head to the side and stared at her pro-file. There was a tiny bump along the ridge of her nose, so small you almost couldn't see it. She wore mascara, but a few blond lashes in the corner had escaped the brush. "I dreamed about rodeo. I wanted to ride bulls and broncs because it was more exciting than going to school and coming home to do chores."

She blinked at him. "And?"

"I followed that dream."

"I heard you were good enough to win a few buckles."

He grinned. "I was."

She turned onto her side and propped her head on her hand. "Do you ever think about competing again?"

"No, but I'm glad I got to chase my dream for a few years before my father passed away." He reached across his chest and toyed with a strand of her blond hair. "What about you?"

"What about me what?" she asked.

"What did you dream of when you were a young girl?"

"My mom called me vintage Sadie because I'd talk about wanting to grow up, get married and be a mother."

"Your dream of being a mother came true," he said.

She lay back down. "Do you know that Lydia, myself and our other cousin, Scarlett, are all only children?"

Logan shook his head.

"We made a pact when we were younger that we'd get married and have lots of kids because we hated growing up without sisters and brothers."

"I think you've fulfilled your end of the deal," he said.

"Don't get me wrong. I love my boys. They exhaust me, frustrate me at times, but I can't imagine my life without them." She smiled. "But I've wondered if having a little girl would help settle Tommy down."

"Maybe if my brothers and I had a sister we'd have been less wild."

"The best part about little girls is that one minute

they're acting all prissy and girlie-girl, and the next they're outside digging in the dirt with the neighbor boys."

"My grandma once said she'd wished one of us boys had been a girl, but it was probably best my parents only had boys. When my grandmother died, Gramps became both mother and father until me and my brothers were old enough to fend for ourselves."

"Solo parenting is rough. Things would be less stressful if Pete lived up to his responsibilities."

Logan reached for her hand and threaded his fingers through hers.

"After the divorce we split the payments for the twins' day care and then preschool. More than half the time Pete would forget to pay his portion or he'd call and ask me to cover his share until he could reimburse me."

"Why'd you bail him out?"

"The first time I didn't, then a few days later when I took the boys to day care we were turned away at the door because Pete hadn't paid."

Logan didn't know what to say. He felt like Sadie had taken a baseball bat and swung it as hard as she could at his gut. He was exactly the kind of guy she didn't need in her life—a guy who, no matter how good his intentions were, would never get his act together.

He thought back to his marriage. Even though Beth had been focused on trying to get pregnant, she'd noticed he'd struggled to keep organized and stay on track. If they'd succeeded in having a baby, he had no idea if they'd still be married or if his ADD would have ended their marriage.

He hadn't asked Sadie to take a walk with him so

he could feel bad about himself. "We'd better get back to the house."

"Wait." Her fingers clamped around his arm. "You said something the other night in the kitchen."

Damn. He should have known he couldn't make a comment like that and not think she'd have questions.

"Why don't you want children?" When he didn't respond immediately, she rushed on, "I mean you're great with the boys. You're a natural father. Patient. Kind. And way more easygoing than I am with my sons."

He owed her the truth—because part of him clung to a tiny sliver of hope that their relationship might develop into something deeper. Something long-term. "The reason Beth and I got divorced was because I'm sterile and she wanted children the old-fashioned way."

He didn't know what kind of reaction he expected from Sadie, but when she leaned her head against his shoulder, his muscles relaxed.

"I'm sorry, Logan. So sorry."

The sincerity in her voice wrapped around him like a warm blanket. When he'd first gotten the news from the doctor, he'd been shocked, then angry. He'd nurtured his anger because he'd known the moment he let his guard down, the sorrow would destroy him. He felt a tickle on his thigh—Sadie's finger caressing the denim, her touch comforting.

"I suggested adoption, but Beth was adamant that she wanted the experience of being pregnant and carrying her own baby."

"What about a sperm donor?"

He shook his head. "She wanted to be married to the father of her child." He was grateful Sadie didn't try to reassure him that someday he'd meet a woman who wouldn't care if he was sterile or who'd be open to adopting. Right now the only woman occupying his thoughts night and day was the one next to him—the one who dreamed of having more children.

"I'd appreciate it if we kept this conversation just between us." He cringed when his voice cracked.

"Your grandfather and brothers have no idea?"

"No." He'd thought about telling Gunner after Lydia had turned up pregnant, but he hadn't wanted to put a damper on their excitement at being expectant parents.

"We'd better head back to the house before your grandfather sends out a search party for us."

Logan climbed to his feet. He reached down and helped Sadie off the ground but didn't release her. "How are the bruises healing?"

"Better," she whispered.

He inhaled her scent—fresh air and a hint of faded perfume. He was attracted to Sadie, and not just physically. There were so many things he admired about her. The courage and stamina it took to raise her sons on her own while working full-time. Her love of family. Her generosity and willingness to help him. Sadie was kind. Grounded. Confident.

And so damned desirable.

He brushed his mouth against hers. Once wasn't enough. The second time their lips touched, he captured her sigh. After she broke off the kiss Logan closed his eyes, relishing the feel of her in his arms. As they finally headed back toward the house, he realized that if he let his guard down around her, she'd have the power to crush his already wounded and battered heart.

A BRIGHT SWATH of light traveled across the wall in the office and Logan glanced toward the doorway where his grandfather stood holding a flashlight. "What's the matter? Trouble sleeping?" he asked the old man.

"I can't sleep most nights, but if I could, all the racket you're making in here would have woken me."

"I'm sorting papers, not tipping over furniture." If Gramps wasn't complaining about something, he wasn't happy.

"What kind of papers?" His grandfather sat on the couch.

"Receipts." Logan had been working since Sadie and the boys left a few hours ago. The one thing he'd discovered about himself since he'd been diagnosed with ADD was that when he was under a lot of pressure to complete a task and time was running out, his anxiety kicked into overdrive. The release of adrenaline into his bloodstream fed his brain and allowed him to push through the urge to procrastinate.

"Sadie's a smart gal. I think she's already got a pretty good idea of where things stand with the bank."

There was no sense trying to pull the wool over the old man's eyes. "It doesn't look good, Gramps." He forced himself to make eye contact. His grandfather looked his age tonight. "Why didn't you tell me you took out a second mortgage?"

"Beef prices had fallen and the ranch was in the red when your grandmother got the bad news about her cancer." Gramps ran his hand over his thinning hair. "The doctors didn't give her much hope even with treatment, but I told her I needed more time to say goodbye. If she'd known I borrowed against the ranch, she would have withdrawn her consent to the treatment." The wrinkles deepened around his mouth. "She suffered longer than she should have because of me."

"She loved you, Gramps."

"When are Sadie and the boys coming out tomorrow?"

"I'm not sure. She didn't say."

"The twins are cute buggers. Tommy reminds me of you. He can't sit still for more than five seconds at a time." His grandfather walked to the doorway. "It's nice having kids run wild again. Sara would have loved being a great-grandmother."

Logan forced a smile, but he felt like throwing up. "Gunner and Lydia will have a little brat tearing around before you know it."

"I'll probably be dead by the time their baby learns to talk."

His grandfather left the room. Logan waited until he heard the sound of the bedroom door close before stepping outside to clear his head. Clenching his hands, he stared at the starlit sky until the ache in his chest dissolved. He'd done nothing his whole life but let people down. The only time he'd felt the rush of victory was when he'd been rodeoing. Even as a kid he'd always been attracted to high-risk activities. He'd thought something was wrong with him until the doctor had explained that it was common for people with ADD to be adrenaline junkies. Bull riding had satisfied his craving for excitement and stimulation. On the circuit, he'd been a winner.

But here at the ranch, and in the eyes of his family, he was a failure.

"WHERE ARE THE BOYS?" Aunt Amelia asked when Sadie walked into the kitchen Thursday morning.

"They're eating their breakfast in the attic. They love sitting at the desks up there." Sadie smiled. "And sitting still is one of the things Tommy doesn't do well, so I figured it wouldn't hurt him to practice."

Amelia made herself a cup of tea and joined Sadie at the table. "I thought while you're working at the ranch today, I'd take the boys out to the Hendersons' farm and we'd pick apples. I'm hoping Emmett will bake a pie for the picnic."

"You're supposed to bring the dessert."

"Emmett knows I can't cook worth a darn."

"How far is the Henderson farm from town?" Sadie asked.

"Fifteen miles." Amelia sipped her tea. "I asked Lydia to come along, and she said yes."

"The boys have never been apple picking. I'm sure they'll have fun." A loud crash sounded above their heads and Sadie held her breath. When no one began yelling or crying, she smiled and said, "So much for sitting still."

"Boys will be boys."

"Aunt Amelia, can I poke around inside your garden shed and see if you have any landscape supplies?"

"I believe there's a few bags of mulch and potting soil left over from spring. What are you planning to do?"

"I thought I'd try to nurse Sara's rosebushes back to life."

Amelia's eyes grew misty. "She would love that."

"Good. I can't wait to get started." Sadie had always found digging in the dirt to be therapeutic. She glanced at the clock, then tossed her purse over her shoulder. "I'll leave the booster seats on the porch."

"We'll drop the twins off at the ranch later this afternoon."

"I'll text Logan and tell him not to expect the boys until later, then." Sadie spent fifteen minutes rummaging through the shed and loading garden supplies into the back of the van before taking off. The drive to Paradise Ranch took only ten minutes after leaving the town limits. When she pulled into the yard, both Emmett's and Logan's pickups were gone. She climbed the porch steps and knocked. No answer. She opened the door and stepped inside. "Anyone home?"

Silence.

There was a full pot of coffee sitting on the counter with a note that said "Help yourself." The horses were in the corral, but there was no sign of the men. Maybe they'd left for only a few minutes and would be back soon. Sadie decided to take advantage of the peace and quiet to tend to Sara's bushes.

A half hour later, shoes dusted with dirt and sweat pouring down her face, Sadie was conducting a therapy session with herself. As she tilled the dirt around the bushes and mixed in the fresh potting soil, she couldn't get her mind off Logan and his confession last night.

Sterile.

The word itself was cold and ugly. The fact that he hadn't shared his diagnosis with his grandfather or brothers told her how deeply it bothered him. She could only imagine how difficult it was for him to witness Gunner's excitement about Lydia's pregnancy. And part of Sadie suspected that Logan had asked her to keep his secret because he didn't want his situation to take away from his brother's and sister-in-law's joy.

She kneaded the heavy clay with her fingers, breaking the hard lumps apart. Her heart ached for Logan. Yes, he had ADD, but that didn't mean he wasn't fit to be a father. She'd seen firsthand how patient, kind and generous he was with her sons. For his sake, she hoped that one day he'd find a woman who would be open to adoption or, if they had the financial means, using a sperm donor.

"Ouch!" Sadie dropped the clump of soil, then pulled off her garden glove and plucked a tiny thorn from her pinkie finger.

Darn you, Logan.

They were adults—old enough to know what it meant to play with fire. So why had he struck a match and kissed her last night.

Because he knows you're attracted to him.

It wasn't difficult to think about Logan as more than a cousin-in-law, but she couldn't allow herself to get too carried away when eventually she and the boys would return to Wisconsin. Even if she and Logan had met in Madison, a long-term relationship with him wouldn't have worked. She didn't need more stress in her life when she dealt with Tommy's ADD every day.

She slipped her hands back into the earth and then opened a bag of mulch and spread it around the base of the bushes. When she envisioned herself married, it wasn't to a man like Logan. She wanted a partner who'd help carry the load, not one who'd upend her efforts to keep their lives organized and on schedule. There were nights she cried herself to sleep from sheer exhaustion after Tommy had a bad day. No man wanted to sleep next to a weepy wife. After a while, the strain would ruin the marriage and she'd be back to square one again—a single mother, only with twice the baggage.

Chapter Nine

Sadie checked the time on her cell phone after she finished snipping the dead canes on the rosebushes. She'd worked nonstop for almost two hours and there was still no sign of the Hardell men.

Feeling relaxed and invigorated after her therapy session with the rosebushes, she washed up at the kitchen sink, then poured herself a cup of coffee and reheated it in the microwave before heading down the hallway to the office. When she opened the door, she froze, her gaze taking in the stacks of papers and receipts lined up in neat rows across the floor.

She'd spent the past two hours convincing herself that a relationship with Logan would only add stress to her life, and then he'd surprised her by not just making a dent in organizing the paperwork, but completing the entire task. She had no idea how he'd managed to accomplish so much in so little time, but he'd opened her eyes to the possibility that maybe he could be the kind of partner she needed, after all.

She shoved the door closed on that thought and set her coffee on the desk before dropping to her knees to examine the sticky notes Logan had used to label the piles—*feed store, household expenses, vet bills, incidentals*, *truck payment*, *taxes* and *bank*, which included statements and correspondence.

A shiver of excitement spread through Sadie. She loved crunching numbers. She carried the papers to the desk and settled into the chair, then turned on the calculator. The next time she looked up from her work, Logan stood in the doorway with lunch.

"HUNGRY?" LOGAN ENTERED the room and set the tray of food on the coffee table before sitting down on the couch.

She glanced at the wall clock. "Two o'clock already?" Sadie moved the calculator aside, stood and stretched.

Logan averted his eyes when the material of her shirt pulled tight over her bosom. After getting no sleep last night and then spending the morning chasing cows, he was loopy enough to do something stupid like pull Sadie into his lap and kiss her.

She sat next to him and helped herself to a sandwich. "Don't tell the boys I didn't wash my hands before eating."

"I won't."

"Thanks for making lunch," she said.

"You're welcome." He took a bite, his taste buds barely registering the tangy flavor of the deli mustard.

"No one was home when I arrived. Where did you and your grandfather go off to?"

"I was loading cattle for transport to a feedlot and Gramps had a meeting with the town council."

"What's going on with the town?"

"Something to do with replacing a broken water pipe in the basement of the old Woolworth building."

He set aside the sandwich, his appetite dwindling at the prospect of learning the ranch's fate.

"If you don't mind," he said, "I'd like to get this over with." His comment wiped the smile off her face. "I don't mean to be rude, Sadie, after all the time you've spent—"

"You've put in just as many hours as I have. And thanks to the work you did last night, things went much faster this morning."

"So how bad is it?" he asked.

"Bad."

The three-letter word shot through his chest like an arrow.

"The bank is within its rights to foreclose on the property."

"And you're sure they gave us the proper notice?"

She nodded. "I found all three late notices."

"I don't remember seeing the letters."

"The envelopes were never opened."

Logan hated the look of pity in her eyes.

"There's other correspondence from the bank that was never opened."

"What kind of correspondence?"

"A demand letter, which basically notifies you that you're late paying your mortgage. It also tells you how far behind you are on the payments and orders you to get current within thirty days." She grasped his arm. "It was dated July first."

Logan wasn't sure if it was Sadie's soft touch or the bad news that caused his heart to lurch in his chest. "Did you find the official letter from the bank saying the ranch is in foreclosure?"

"That's the interesting thing… I haven't." She offered a small smile. "I'm thinking the bank is holding off taking any further action because someone has called in a favor on your behalf."

"Amelia's the reason we haven't lost the ranch yet." He clasped his hands together. "Where does that leave me?"

"I'd tell you to make up the missed payments and pay off the accumulated interest, but after looking over your bank deposits, you don't have enough money or assets to do that."

"Unless I win the lottery it appears the only way out of this mess is to accept your aunt's offer to settle our debt."

"I don't see another way out."

A car pulled up outside and Sadie stood. "That's Lydia and my aunt. They took the twins to an apple farm today."

Logan followed her outside and waited on the front porch while Sadie helped the boys out of the car, and then removed their booster seats. The twins each held a small cloth bag filled with fruit.

"Uncle Logan, we picked apples." Tommy rushed forward but tripped over his feet and upended his bag, sending apples rolling in all directions. Tyler helped his brother put the apples back into the bag and then the boys climbed the porch steps.

Logan made a big production of examining an apple from each bag. "Looks like you two picked the best ones on the farm."

"Where's Gramps?" Tommy asked.

"He went into town for a while. He'll be back shortly."

"Boys," Sadie said, "thank Aunt Lydia and Aunt Amelia for taking you apple picking."

"Thank you, Aunt Lydia and Aunt Amelia!"

"Why don't you guys take the apples into the kitchen." Logan held the door open and as soon as the twins went into the house, he descended the steps and approached the women, prepared to eat humble pie.

Lydia excused herself to use the bathroom and went into the house, leaving Logan alone with Sadie and Amelia.

"Where are we with examining the ranch accounts?" Amelia asked.

Sadie opened her mouth to respond, but Logan jumped in, not wanting her to make more excuses for him. "I'll need a few more days to get Gramps on board with your idea," he said.

"So we have a deal?" Amelia asked.

"We have a deal." His grandfather wouldn't like it, but his name wasn't on the title to the property and Logan had no other option if he wanted Paradise Ranch to stay in the Hardell family. "On behalf of my grandfather and brothers…thank you for your generosity."

"You can thank me by making sure Emmett stays involved with the project."

Great. The old woman was going to pull their strings every which way until he and his grandfather were tied in knots. "Stay involved how?"

"Emmett's turned into a cranky old man the past few years—" Logan couldn't argue with that "—and I'm hoping you can persuade him to help run the petting zoo or manage the trail rides. He could use some work on his social skills."

Logan suspected Amelia's idea to bring tourists to the ranch was about helping his grandfather more than the local economy.

Sadie touched Logan's arm. "Would you send Lydia out here and keep an eye on the boys until I come in?"

"Sure." Logan went into the house and delivered the message to Lydia. Left alone in the kitchen with the boys, who munched on their apples, he asked, "Did you guys wash those before you started eating them?"

"Aunt Lydia did," Tyler said.

"How would you like to clean the rest of the apples for Gramps so he can use them to make pies?" Logan pushed two chairs over to the counter, put the stopper in the drain and filled the sink with warm water. "Dump your apples in here and swish them around," he said.

The boys climbed onto the chairs and unloaded their bags, the apples plopping into the water and splashing their shirts.

"Swim 'em around, Tyler," Tommy said.

The back door opened and Logan's grandfather stepped into the kitchen.

"We're swimming apples," Tommy called over his shoulder.

"Swishing," Logan corrected.

Gramps peered into the sink. "Those are some mighty fine apples."

"Aunt Amelia said you're gonna make pies with our apples," Tyler said.

"She did, huh?" His grandfather chuckled. "That's because your aunt Amelia loves my apple pie."

"How'd things go with the city council?" Logan asked.

"We're replacing all the plumbing in the basement of the building. Doesn't make sense to fix one pipe and not the rest when they're all old." He nodded to the twins. "Have fun, boys, I'm gonna catch a nap before supper."

"Amelia's out front," Logan said.

"I know. Why'd you think I came in the back door?"

Logan watched his grandfather skulk out of the room. Amelia was right about the old man needing an attitude adjustment.

"What are we gonna do now?" Tommy jumped down from the chair.

"You two know what a tree house is?" Logan asked.

The boys shook their heads.

"What do you do in a tree house?" Tyler asked.

"Lots of stuff. You can play games, have sleepovers, read books or hide." Logan narrowed his eyes. "I've got just the tree in mind. Do you guys want to help me build a house?"

The boys looked at each other, then nodded.

"Okay, then. We have a lot of work to do before dark." He led them outside and across the yard to the barn. They made several trips from the storage room to the truck, carrying hammers, boxes of nails and screws. He loaded the cordless drill, a handsaw and a pair of folding sawhorses.

"That's a lot of stuff." Tyler stared at the truck bed.

"Stand back while I bring out the wood." There were several mismatched boards from previous construction projects on the ranch stored in the back of the barn. He picked the best ones, then tossed a canvas tarp into the pickup. "Almost ready." He filled a cooler with water from the hose and set it on the back seat, then opened the passenger-side door and helped Tommy and Tyler into the front seat, pulling the belt across both their laps and then moving the shoulder strap behind them.

Logan climbed in behind the wheel. "We're not even going a half mile, so I don't think your mom will mind if you sit in the front seat." He drove behind the house, then turned onto the dirt path he and Sadie had walked along when he'd shown her his childhood hiding place. Twenty yards farther he hit the brakes. "We're here." He helped the boys out of the pickup and asked, "Which tree do you like best?" He pointed to a pair of live oaks.

The brothers looked confused. Logan walked over to the biggest tree with the thickest branches. "What about this one?" They all studied the tree, which had a lower hanging limb that appeared sturdy. It would take only four steps nailed to the trunk for the boys to reach the first limb, which wasn't that far off the ground. Maybe when they grew older he could build a second story higher up.

Second story? There he went again thinking the twins would be around every day and not just every once in a while when Sadie visited her cousin and aunt in Stampede.

"The first thing we need to do is nail boards against the trunk so you can climb up." He glanced down and made eye contact with only one pair of blue eyes—Tyler's. He looked behind him. Tommy was hunched down, drawing in the dirt with a stick.

"You ready for your first task?" he asked Tyler. The boy nodded. "Help me unload the supplies, then you can pound a few nails." Keeping a close eye on

Tommy, Logan hauled the materials over to the base of the tree, then took out the cooler and placed it in the shade.

"Hey, Tommy!" When the kid glanced up, Logan said, "Don't wander off, okay?" He didn't trust him not to become distracted by a butterfly and chase after it. He set up the sawhorses and worked facing the boy so he could keep an eye on him.

"Hold the end of this board, Tyler." Logan used a handsaw to cut three sections of wood two feet long. "Now we nail these to the trunk to make the steps." He drove in the first few nails, then handed the hammer to Tyler and helped him pound two more into the wood. "Good job. Time to test our handiwork." He lifted Tyler onto the first step. "Climb up and sit on the lower branch."

"Look, Tommy!" Tyler waved.

When Tommy saw his brother in the tree, he raced over to Logan's side. "Can I go up there, too?"

Logan let Tommy climb up and sit for a minute before he lowered the boys to the ground. "Next, we build the floor."

"I'm bored." Tommy squinted at Logan.

"You guys sit in the shade and watch."

The boys did as he asked and Logan worked at lightning speed cutting boards and plywood to fit between the tree branches. He used lag screws and washers to secure the main supports before laying down the floor. When he finished, he walked across the wood, making sure it could hold his weight.

Tommy raced over to the tree. "Is it ready?"

"Not until I make the walls." Logan jumped to the ground. "You'll have to wait a little longer."

He and his brothers had built several forts through the years and none of them had had rails, but he doubted Sadie would let the twins play in a tree at their age without them. He nailed two-by-fours along the sides, enclosing the area.

"I need you boys to help me with the roof." He removed the canvas tarp from the pickup. "Climb into the fort and hold one side while I nail down the other." The boys did as he asked and Logan secured the material above their heads. "What do you think of your new tree house?"

"Can I read in here?" Tyler asked.

"Sure," Logan said.

"Does a tree house have ghosts?" Tyler asked.

"Nope. Ghosts aren't allowed."

"What about Bruiser?"

Logan stared at Tyler. "Who's Bruiser?"

"You know," Tommy said. "Bruiser the bear."

The imaginary bear his grandfather had told stories about when he'd taken the boys fishing.

"Yeah," Tyler said. "Is Bruiser gonna find us?"

"Bruiser is long gone," Logan said.

"What about monsters?" Tommy asked.

Logan shook his head. "No monsters."

"I wanna sleep up here," Tommy said.

If Sadie agreed to let the boys spend a night in the woods, Logan would have to camp out in his truck and make sure no bogeyman showed up.

Tommy descended the steps. "Let's go tell Mom, Tyler."

"I need help putting this stuff back into the truck bed," Logan said.

Once the supplies and tools were stowed away, Tommy asked, "Can I drive your truck?"

Logan made a big production of looking shocked. "You mean you guys have never driven before?" Their heads shook back and forth. Logan had sat on his grandfather's lap behind the wheel of a tractor at the age of three.

He set the boys in the front seat and the cooler in the back, then got behind the wheel. "One at a time."

Tommy climbed onto his lap and gripped the wheel. Logan started the engine, then shifted into Reverse, his left foot hovering over the brake. "Turn the wheel to the right."

"Where's right?" Tommy asked.

Tyler pointed out the windshield to his right. "That way." The boy was whip smart.

Tommy steered and Logan applied just enough pressure on the gas pedal until the truck swung around and faced the direction they'd come in. "Straighten it out." He helped Tommy move the wheel into position. "Hold steady so we stay on the road."

"Can I have a turn?" Tyler asked.

Tommy looked at Logan. "Go faster."

"We're going fast enough." He spoke to Tyler. "As soon as we get to the end of the road, you can take us the rest of the way back to the barn."

Tyler's face split into a grin.

Logan got a kick out of their excitement and then in the next instant he realized how lonely it was going to be around the ranch if he couldn't convince Sadie to remain in Stampede with the boys.

EARLY THURSDAY EVENING, Sadie sat on the wrap-around front porch of her aunt's home waiting for her cousin to arrive. The house sat on the corner of Buckaroo Avenue and Vaquero Lane and stuck out like a sore thumb among the single-story homes around it. The yellow blooms on the butterfly vine covering the wrought iron fence, which enclosed the yard, had faded. She smiled at the large magnolia tree, remembering the numerous games of tag she and her cousins had played around it. Pink blossoms from the crepe myrtle trees littered the driveway and the Boston ferns hanging along the porch looked thirsty and tired of battling the summer heat. But the small pot of daisies sitting on the table between a pair of white rockers at the end of the porch was still bright and cheery. "Thanks for coming over," Sadie said when Lydia walked up the sidewalk and sat next to her on the porch steps.

"It beats watching baseball with Gunner." Lydia laughed. "He closed the motel for a couple of hours to watch the game at the bar in town."

"You two seem really happy."

"He's not at all the kind of man I envisioned for myself, but you can't choose who you fall in love with."

Sadie mulled over her cousin's words. She'd thought she'd been in love with Pete and they'd tried to make it work, but in the end it had been impossible. "I've been thinking a lot about the future."

"Does this mean you're considering staying in Stampede or somewhere nearby?"

Sadie nodded. "Where to live hasn't been the only thing on my mind lately."

"Logan?"

"Is it that obvious that I'm attracted to him?"

Lydia nodded. "Let's take a trip down memory lane."

They left the porch and walked to the corner, then crossed the street and strolled along Chuck Wagon Drive, the main thoroughfare.

"You've been spending a lot of time out at the ranch—" Lydia smiled "—not working."

"The boys are having so much fun hanging around Logan and Emmett." They passed by the old Woolworth, which had closed its doors decades ago. The building now housed the Cattle Drive Café, a library and Statewide Insurance.

"What about you?" Lydia said. "Aunt Amelia put you to work as soon as you got here. It hasn't been much of a vacation."

"Strangely enough I haven't felt this relaxed in months. I might be holed up inside the ranch office for several hours a day, but not having to deal with co-worker gossip, a long commute and Tommy's teacher complaining about his behavior has been a huge relief."

They passed by the Saddle Up Saloon, where Gunner's truck sat parked in the street. They continued walking until they reached the Buckets of Suds coin-operated laundry. An out-of-business sign hung in the window.

Sadie poked her cousin in the arm. "Remember when Scarlett puked in her sleeping bag and Aunt Amelia gave us a bunch of quarters, then sent us down here to wash it?"

"We put too much soap in the machine and bubbles got all over the floor."

"What was the name of the manager?"

"Mr. Bell," Lydia said.

"He made us girls mop the floor." They moved on past Lydia and Gunner's apartment. "I want the boys to have fun memories like ours, but they won't get them living away from their cousins."

"It sounds like you're looking for a slower-paced life," Lydia said.

"It's what I want for me and the boys, but I don't know if it's what I can have. If Tommy gets accepted into that special preschool, I'll be back to square one again, dealing with commutes, carpools and extra-curricular activities."

"Have the boys mentioned that they miss playing soccer?" Lydia asked.

"Not once. They're having too much fun running around at the ranch." Sadie nibbled her lower lip.

"Why do I get the feeling there's more to worrying about the future than just where to live?"

"I like Logan. A lot," Sadie said.

"More than a lot?"

"Maybe. And it frightens me."

They reached the end of the block and crossed the street to the old Amoco filling station, which had been converted into a vegetable stand. Lydia pointed to the bench in front of the window and they sat. "What are you afraid of? Logan's great with the boys. And you won't find a man who cares more about family than him."

"You don't know, do you?" Sadie asked.

"Know what?"

Sadie would never tell a stranger about Logan's

private issues, but Lydia had been sympathetic and supportive when she'd told her cousin about her son's disorder. "Logan has ADD, just like Tommy."

"Really?" Lydia shrugged. "I probably haven't been around him enough to pick up on it." She snapped her fingers. "Wait. The night you arrived in town with the boys, Logan was manning the front desk at the motel and I remember Gunner telling me later the next day that Logan had mixed up the billing invoices and Gunner had to redo them." Lydia sucked in a quick breath. "Is that why the bank is threatening to foreclose on the ranch? Logan messed up the finances?"

Sadie nodded. "It's difficult enough watching out for Tommy. If my partner requires the same supervision, I'll be exhausted all the time. And then what if I grow resentful because I feel like I'm doing all the work or cleaning up all the messes? If it got to be too much, I'd yell and then feel guilty because Logan can't help it that he has ADD."

"I can't pretend to understand how that would feel, but can you give the guy credit for trying? Celebrate when he succeeds and roll with the punches when he makes a mess of things."

Lydia made it sound easy, but she had no experience living with someone with ADD 24/7.

"Don't overthink things," Lydia said. "If you fall in love, worry about it then."

"Sound advice. C'mon." Sadie took her cousin's arm. "I'll buy you an ice cream at the café. Then you can tell me what baby names you and Gunner are considering."

"We've already picked out names, but they're a secret."

"I spill my guts and you get to keep secrets." Sadie laughed. "You always were the smart cousin."

Chapter Ten

"You got a minute to talk?" Logan stepped onto the front porch, where his grandfather had taken a seat once they'd said goodbye to Sadie and the boys after supper.

"Take a load off." Gramps nodded to the rocking chair next to him, and Logan sat.

"Sadie trimmed the rosebushes and put down mulch." He pointed to the cleaned-up garden bed. "Your grandmother would like Sadie."

Logan agreed.

"Be nice to have a woman's touch around this old place again." His grandfather eyed Logan. "What's on your mind?"

There was no sense waiting to tell his grandfather he'd failed. He might as well rip off the bandage and come clean.

"I screwed up."

"How's that?"

"I let things slip. I didn't pay attention to the bills the way I should have." His grandfather opened his mouth to speak, but Logan cut him off. "When you asked me to quit rodeo and run the ranch, I wasn't happy about it."

"I knew that."

"I'm not proud to admit that I resented Gunner and Reid because you didn't ask for their help."

His grandfather stared into space for a long while, then cleared his throat. "I shouldn't have put it all on your shoulders."

"I was the eldest, so it made sense that you'd want me at the reins, but I was still pissed and that anger festered inside me, messed with my head, and it made it even more difficult to keep track of the ranch accounts."

"What do you mean?"

"Some nights I'd come in from the barn tired as hell and I knew I had to open mail, pay bills or enter receipts into the checkbook and I'd tell myself I'd do it later, or I'd set the bills in one pile, thinking I'd get to them in the morning, and then the next day I'd have another excuse and move the pile somewhere else to remind me later." He drew in a deep breath and exhaled. "You said Tommy reminded you of me when I was young."

"He does."

"That's because I have ADD, Gramps, just like Tommy. I have a tough time keeping things organized and staying focused."

His grandfather's eyes widened. "Why didn't you say something?"

"I was embarrassed." When the doctor had said *ADD*, Logan had been ashamed because he'd associated the diagnosis with kids, not adults. Even though the doctor had explained that adults also suffered from the condition, he'd seen it as weakness.

"I should have helped more," Gramps said. "I was in a bad place after your dad died."

"I know, Gramps. This isn't your fault. I could have asked for help when I got in over my head, but I tried to handle it myself."

Logan had been late paying the mortgage and other bills at times, but he'd caught the mistakes before any real damage had been done. Receiving an official diagnosis of ADD this past spring had sent him in a downward spiral and the important things had slipped through the cracks without him noticing.

Logan dragged a hand down his face. "I've missed more than a couple of mortgage payments."

His grandfather's gaze fixated on the rosebushes.

"Sadie said the bank followed all the rules and it's within their right to foreclose on the ranch."

Gramps nodded.

"She couldn't find any documentation to prove that they've begun the foreclosure process. I think Amelia's the reason why we haven't lost this place." When his grandfather remained silent, he said, "If there was another way out of this mess I'd tell you to take it, but if we want to keep the property in the family we have to accept Amelia's offer."

"We could sell the rest of the herd."

"We don't have enough cows to pay off the debt." Logan paced across the porch. "If we let her help, we'll be in the black again. There's always a chance this trail ride and petting zoo will be a success and the added income would provide us with more financial security."

"That woman's a shyster."

"What do you mean?" Logan asked.

"Don't you see?" Gramps said. "In exchange for her paying off our debts, she gets to tell us what to do with our property. That woman isn't happy unless she's sticking her nose in other people's business."

Logan would find out just how much say Amelia wanted in the project when he spoke to her. "Think you can handle your old girlfriend bossing us around?"

His grandfather made a rude noise. "Been letting her get away with it since Sara died."

It sounded like Gramps was coming around to Amelia's deal.

"The boys would get a kick out of having baby animals to play with," his grandfather said. Maybe Logan wasn't the only Hardell man imagining the twins staying in Stampede forever.

Gramps rubbed his whiskers. "I guess it's not hard to feed and water a few more animals every day, but who's going to keep track of the finances?"

It was a fair question. His grandfather didn't want to accept Amelia's help only to end up in the same financial mess down the road. "Sadie said she'd teach me how to use the business software she downloaded to the computer, but to be safe we can hire a part-time bookkeeper or accountant to catch anything I miss." Logan cleared his throat. "I'm sorry I let you down, Gramps."

"What's done is done, grandson."

"I'll speak to Amelia at the picnic and tell her that we're signing on to her plans." Logan should be the one to eat crow, not his grandfather.

"Maybe the boys can ride along with us when we pick out the baby animals," Gramps said.

"The twins are a lot of work."

"No more than you and your brothers were. Your

grandmother ran herself ragged trying to keep up with you kids."

"Did it bother you that our parents shrugged off their responsibility for us?"

"Sure it did. Your grandmother and I did our best, but you boys needed your mother and father."

"Gunner missed Mom the most and Reid was closest to Dad because they loved working on cars together."

Gramps stared at Logan. "You were always left out."

It was Logan's turn to study the rosebushes. "I wasn't exactly an easy kid."

"The boys couldn't stop talking about the tree house you built for them."

"Tyler wants to read his books out there and Tommy wants to have a sleepover."

"It'll be lonely around here when they leave."

His grandfather's words weighed heavy on Logan's heart. He'd miss the boys, too.

"You and Beth didn't last long enough to have kids." Gramps pointed his finger at Logan. "You better get a move on and find a gal or Gunner and Lydia will have a handful of rascals running wild by the time you have your first."

The knot in Logan's chest dropped to his stomach. He'd love to have kids someday, but it wouldn't be the old-fashioned way.

"Maybe you should set your sights on Sadie."

Logan's head whipped sideways and his grandfather chuckled.

"I've seen the way you watch that gal when you think no one's looking."

Logan struggled not to laugh. "I don't badger you about your love life."

Gramps sputtered. "I don't have a love life."

"If you think you're doing a good job of hiding your feelings for Amelia, then you're only fooling yourself."

"You're talking nonsense, boy."

"What happened between the two of you years ago?"

The lines in his grandfather's face relaxed. "We dated in high school."

"Why'd you break up?"

"I can't remember, but Amelia was always opinionated and bossy." He grinned. "I liked that about her when she was younger."

Logan got the sense Amelia's stubbornness still amused his grandfather, though the old man refused to admit it.

"I figured once she was done pouting, we'd patch things up."

"But you didn't?"

"It was too late." Gramps's smile flipped upside down. "She met Robert and he sweet-talked her into his bed." Gramps shifted in the rocker. "Sara, Amelia and me were all best friends in school. Sara was the one who told me that Robert had gotten Amelia pregnant."

"What happened to Amelia's baby?" Logan had never seen or heard of the older woman's child.

"She miscarried, and she and Robert never had any kids."

That explained why Amelia was close to her great-nieces. He touched his grandfather's arm. "Did Grandma know you pined after Amelia?"

"I stopped pining once I married Sara. Amelia pushed us together and I'm glad she did." He nodded. "I loved Sara. She was a good woman, and she put up with me despite all my faults."

"But you never loved her the way you loved Amelia."

Gramps shook his head.

"Is that why you borrowed money from Amelia to buy the motel for Grandma? Because you felt guilty?"

"Yes."

"And guilt was the reason you went against Grandma's wishes to fight her cancer and took out that second mortgage to get her the best treatment possible?"

"Yes."

"Despite what happened between you and Amelia, Grandma knew you loved her."

"I'll talk to Amelia at the picnic."

"Thanks, Gramps, but this is my doing. I'll handle it."

"What are your plans for Sadie and the boys?"

"What do you mean by plans?"

"You like her, don't you?"

"Yes."

"Then don't let any grass grow under your feet or she'll be gone before you know it."

Gramps's advice was sound. Logan had to give Sadie a reason to stay in Stampede.

His grandfather stood. "When it's all said and done, grandson, we only regret the chances we didn't take."

Logan remained on the porch long after the old man went into the house. He wouldn't deny that Beth's divorcing him had left him feeling inadequate and less a man. To deal with the hurt he'd convinced himself that he wasn't meant to be a father. Then Sadie and the twins had dropped into his life, forcing him to acknowledge that, no matter what he'd told himself in the past, he still yearned to be a dad—even if it meant raising another man's children.

Since he was having a heart-to-heart chat with himself, he might as well admit that his feelings for Sadie were more serious than he'd allowed himself to believe. Aside from being attracted to her, he appreciated that she was caring and sympathetic. And because she had a child with ADD, she understood what made him tick in ways other women would never be able to. She and the boys were the best things to happen to him in a long time. Now the big question was how to convince her that he was the best thing to happen to her and her sons.

"WHEN WILL GUNNER be here?" Sadie asked Lydia Sunday afternoon at the ranch as they sat at the picnic table in the yard.

Aunt Amelia and Emmett were in the kitchen making a pitcher of Kool-Aid for the boys and Logan was grooming the horses while the twins sat on the corral rail and watched.

"He'll be here soon," Lydia said. "The motel filled up last night. This is the first time since the renovation that we didn't have a vacancy."

"I'm not surprised. You did an amazing job with the place and the playroom at Aunt Amelia's. Every night I have to threaten the boys with a time-out to coax them to come down from the attic and get ready for bed."

"You could let them sleep up there."

"You think like a four-year-old." Sadie laughed. "The boys have been begging to have a sleepover in the tree house Logan built."

"Speaking of Logan," Lydia said. "I suggested that Gunner should take time to get to know his nephews while they're here, and he grew defensive."

"Why?" Sadie asked.

"He said all the twins talk about is their *uncle Logan.*" Lydia smiled. "I know that a good preschool is important for Tommy, but I was thinking that you could probably find one in San Antonio and that's closer to Stampede than Madison."

Lydia glanced at the back door, making sure no one eavesdropped on the conversation. "I guess I could do a little research while I'm here with the boys." If Tommy didn't get into the special school in Madison next semester, there was no reason to return to Wisconsin and she could begin looking for other options for her son.

"How are the boys adjusting to Pete not being around anymore?"

"Tyler was quiet on the drive to Texas, but..." Sadie shifted on the bench so she faced the corral. "Ever since we've been here, he hasn't read as much and he and Tommy are getting along better."

"What about Tommy?"

Sadie spread her arms wide. "There are so many distractions on the ranch that he doesn't have time to think about his father leaving."

"I noticed Tyler wasn't as shy when me and Aunt Amelia took the boys apple picking."

"Logan's been a great influence on the boys," Sadie said.

"Has he had a positive influence on you?"

"You couldn't have landed a nicer guy for a brother-in-law." Sadie watched Logan tip his head back and laugh at something Tommy said. He was more patient with the boys than their own father. "He's a nice man."

"Ouch." Lydia cringed. "A *nice* man?"

"It's not smart to think about him any other way."

"Why? There's no man in your life right now, unless you've been holding out on me."

"I haven't been holding out on anyone." Sadie didn't like to have to defend herself—mostly because she was challenging her reasons for keeping Logan at a distance.

"He's not selfish like Pete," Lydia said. "He gave up rodeo to help his grandfather run the ranch."

Logan walked away from an activity that he'd succeeded at. That had reinforced his confidence and made him feel worthy. And he'd traded that for a job where each and every day his faults and shortcomings were thrown in his face. Only a man who put his family ahead of himself would do that. There was no arguing that Logan would make a great father, just not a great partner.

Their conversation about Logan ended when Aunt Amelia and Emmett came out of the house with the pitcher of Kool-Aid and plastic cups.

"Will you girls help me with the food?" Aunt Amelia asked.

"I'll tell the boys to wash up." Emmett walked off.

Fifteen minutes later everyone was seated around the picnic table eating fried chicken, potato salad, homemade mac and cheese, beans, fruit salad and potato chips. Sadie sat across from Lydia and her cousin-in-law and tried to ignore the way Gunner was always touching Lydia—either playing with her hair, leaning into her or putting his arm around her.

Aunt Amelia sat at one end of the table and Emmett at the other, shooting barbs and sharing stories of growing up in Stampede. The boys were sandwiched between Sadie and Logan, but that didn't stop her from looking his way and catching his heated stare. In a perfect world, the four of them could be a real family.

Emmett dropped his napkin on his plate. "You boys want a ride in the Radio Flyer?"

"Logan and I want a ride, too." Gunner grinned.

Amelia rolled her eyes. "Why are the ladies always stuck doing the dishes?"

"Leave the dishes in the sink. I'll wash them later," Emmett said.

Logan hung behind. "Amelia, mind if I have a word with you?"

"Guess that leaves you and me to put the food away." Lydia looked at Sadie before carrying two serving bowls into the house.

"I'd like to check on your grandmother's rosebushes." Amelia led the way to the front yard and Logan followed.

Sadie's heart pinched as she watched the pair walk off. Logan was conceding defeat and her heart ached for him.

"WHO HUNG SARA'S SWING?" Amelia asked, climbing the porch steps.

"I brought it down from the attic and put it up yesterday." Logan leaned against the porch rail, waiting for Sadie's aunt to make herself comfortable.

"Your grandmother loved sitting out here and

watching the sun set." Amelia's gaze shifted to the yard. "I'm glad Sadie pruned the rosebushes."

"Grandma loved her flowers."

The old woman's gaze softened. "You didn't bring me out here to talk about the landscaping."

"No, ma'am, I didn't." Even though his grandfather had accepted Amelia's idea for the ranch, it was tougher than Logan expected to admit he'd failed. He looked away from the pity in her eyes. "I discussed the situation with my grandfather and we'll accept your help paying off the bank in exchange for using a portion of the ranch for trail rides and a petting zoo."

"That's a wise decision."

And a painful one. "When would you like to meet at the bank?"

"Tuesday morning as soon as it opens," she said.

Amelia wasn't wasting any time. "How soon were you planning to begin this project?" he asked.

"Immediately."

Figures she'd want to hit the ground running.

"I want to move quickly before Sadie and the boys return to Wisconsin. I'd like to ask her to oversee the financial end of the project until construction is completed."

The old woman had won him over with that idea.

"Hiring professionals will help move things along."

"I thought you'd want Gramps and me to do most of the work and save you some money." Did she think he'd screw that up, too?

"Money's not a problem. I'm counting on you and Emmett to supervise the work and make sure things are done the right way." She snapped her fingers.

"Emmett said you would take care of selecting the animals for the petting zoo."

Logan nodded.

"He thinks it's a good idea to take the twins with you to test the animals' temperament," she said.

Apparently Amelia and his grandfather had discussed the project at length while they'd been preparing the picnic food.

"You know, Emmett made a good point. If the animals can tolerate Tommy's rambunctiousness, they should be fine around other children who might agitate them."

Logan stuck a finger in his ear and wiggled it, thinking he wasn't hearing Amelia correctly. She talked about his grandfather as if he was a reasonable man and not the stubborn old fool she always called him.

While she droned on about the kind of animals she wanted for the zoo, Logan's mind wandered to Sadie. If she agreed to remain in Stampede and help her aunt's special project, he'd have more time to convince her that she and the boys needed him.

"Tyler and Tommy told me about the tree house you built for them."

"It's not much of a tree house," he said. "I nailed a few boards together and threw a canvas tarp over the top."

"Tyler asked Sadie if he and his brother could have a sleepover there, but she's worried the boys will wear out their welcome at the ranch."

"Gramps likes having the twins around."

"I haven't seen your grandfather as amenable as he's been today in ages."

"He's not such a bad guy," Logan said.

"I've always thought highly of Emmett. I admire the way he took care of Sara when she fell ill." Amelia stared into space. "He swallowed his pride when he came to me for a loan to buy the motel for her. Your grandmother was a very lucky woman to have spent the majority of her life with him."

"Gramps might not seem appreciative of all you've done for us, but he admires you."

Amelia blinked rapidly and turned away. "I wish he'd feel more than admiration."

"I believe he does," Logan said. It was nuts that the pair tiptoed around when it was obvious their feelings for each other hadn't thawed since breaking up in high school. "I don't know all the details about your relationship with my grandfather decades ago, but it's plain as day that he cares for you."

"Hey, you two." Sadie stepped onto the front porch. "Time for dessert. Emmett's boasting about his apple pie." Sadie looked at her aunt. "He said you'd vouch for him that his pie is the best in Texas."

"If that man could, he'd boast himself right out of his pants." Amelia went inside, leaving Sadie alone with Logan.

"I think I'll wait on the pie for a little bit." He smiled. "Feel like taking a walk?" The tightness in his chest eased when she smiled.

"Show me this amazing tree house you built for the twins."

He held out his hand and Sadie slipped her fingers through his. When he touched her, he felt invincible—almost whole again. They walked around the front of the house, cut through the trees and took the dirt path that led to the tree house.

"It's right around the corner," he said.

"This is practically shouting distance from the ranch yard." She stopped when the tree house came into view. "That's why you chose this spot, isn't it?"

"I thought when the boys were a little older they might want to have a sleepover out here and I wanted it to be close enough to the house so you wouldn't worry."

"You probably think I'm overprotective of my sons."

"I think you love your boys and want to do everything in your power to keep them safe."

"Pete thought I hovered too much, but I had no one to share the responsibility of keeping them safe. It's a scary burden to shoulder by yourself."

"You're a great mother, Sadie. Don't let anyone tell you otherwise."

Logan grasped her elbow and guided her over to the tree. "You go up first." He followed her and they sat beneath the tarp.

"You know it's not just Tyler who's changed since we arrived in Stampede," she said. "I've changed, too."

"How?" Logan rubbed his thumb across the back of Sadie's hand, glad she was opening up to him.

"When the boys are happy, I'm less stressed and I feel like I'm a better mother." She smiled at him. "I've never seen them this content and happy, and it's just since we began coming out to the ranch every day."

"Boys love the outdoors," he said.

"It's more than that, Logan."

When Sadie stared into his eyes, he could easily imagine sharing his life with her and the twins.

"My sons are happy because you make them a priority when they're here. They never feel as if they're in the way."

He leaned in and kissed Sadie, because he'd been dying to kiss her all afternoon and because she knew just what to say to make him feel like he mattered.

Logan ended the kiss when he heard his brother calling him. He and Sadie climbed down from the tree, and as they walked back to the ranch yard Sadie said, "I think you should build a tree house for adults."

He chuckled. "I might just do that."

Chapter Eleven

"Yes, I understand." Sadie spoke into her cell phone after helping her aunt clear the breakfast dishes. "Will I get my deposit back?" She listened to the preschool manager explain why she'd only receive a prorated amount. "Would you please mail the check to Texas?" She recited her aunt's address.

The administrator asked if Sadie would wait on the line while she typed the information into the computer. "Sure, I'll hold."

It hadn't taken much effort on Amelia's part to convince Sadie to help set up the business accounts and oversee the financial end of the tourist attraction project at Paradise Ranch. Helping Logan and his grandfather get off on the right foot was one way she could thank them for treating her sons kindly and making their stay in Stampede memorable. And since she didn't have any idea how long her services would be needed, she'd decided to officially withdraw the boys from preschool and save the money she'd been paying to keep their spots for when they returned. If Tommy didn't get into the specialized program for kids with ADD, then she'd consider Lydia's idea and check into preschools in San Antonio. Because deep down Sadie sensed she wasn't ready to say goodbye to Logan, and neither were the twins.

Since they'd arrived in Texas, the boys had quit asking questions about Pete and his new family. When she tucked them into bed at night, all they talked about were Logan and Gramps. Her sons were thriving in Stampede and soaking up the attention from the Hardell men.

Elevator music filled her ears. Sadie didn't understand how it could take more than a few minutes to type in an address—more time for her to daydream about Logan. Her heart ached over the financial mess he and his grandfather were in. As the eldest grandson he hadn't gotten a fair shake, and she agreed with Lydia that he should be appreciated for putting his family before his rodeo career. Admiration aside, he was a handsome man and each night when she turned out the light, the image of that shining water droplet sliding down his bare chest popped into her mind. What would it be like to make love with Logan? Sadie squirmed when her body tingled in places that had been cold for so long.

"Thank you for holding, Ms. McHenry. Everything is taken care of. You should receive a refund within two weeks. Best of luck to you and the boys."

"Thank you for your help." Sadie disconnected the call as her aunt walked into the kitchen.

"I'm on my way to the bank," Amelia said. "I just got off the phone with Logan. He's already there." Her aunt retrieved her purse from the counter. "Logan invited you and the boys to tag along with him to see about a miniature horse that's for sale."

"For the petting zoo?"

Amelia nodded.

"The boys would love that, but aren't we moving a little fast? You and I haven't discussed a budget. And we need to get Logan's and Emmett's input on what upgrades need to be made to the property before any animals are brought to the ranch."

"It's one little horse, dear." Her aunt smiled. "Besides, this will help boost Logan's spirits after our business with the bank."

"When you put it that way, how can the twins and I refuse?"

Amelia nodded. "As far as a budget is concerned, the sky is the limit. I can't take your uncle's oil money with me when I die." She waved a hand in the air. "And don't worry, there will be plenty left over for you girls."

"We're not expecting you to leave us an inheritance. It was more than generous of you to help us pay our college loans."

"You girls are like daughters to me and I couldn't be more happy to leave the three of you a little nest egg after I'm gone."

Sadie got up from the chair and gave her aunt a bear hug. "If money is no object, then I'm going to make sure we don't cut corners, and I'll budget extra money for landscape improvements around the property."

"More rosebushes?"

Sadie nodded. "Emmett mentioned that Sara had a huge vegetable garden on the side of the house. I think he'd approve if I brought the garden back to life. I might plant a few rows of pumpkins so the kids visiting the petting zoo in the fall can pick one out."

"Ask Emmett what he thinks about offering hayrides," Amelia said. "He used to love driving a tractor, but after they quit growing hay they sold the equipment."

"Aren't tractors expensive?"

Her aunt quirked a silver eyebrow and Sadie laughed. "Okay. You don't have to tell me twice. Money is no object."

Amelia opened the back door. "I'll send Logan by the house to pick you up once we finish our business."

"What should we do about supper?" Sadie asked.

"You're on your own. I have dinner plans with friends and won't be home until late."

The door closed and Sadie left the kitchen, stopping at the bottom of the staircase in the foyer. "Boys?"

The twins' feet pounded on the attic steps and a few seconds later they appeared on the landing.

"How would you like to help Logan pick out a new pony?"

"How come she looks so sad?" Tyler asked.

Logan hid his dismay when he got his first glimpse of the miniature horse in the barn stall. The classified ad in the *Stampede Jotter* hadn't mentioned the animal was ancient and neglected.

"How old is she?" Logan asked Melissa Carpenter— her father owned the rural property outside of Rocky Point.

Melissa's gaze skirted Logan's. "I don't know her exact age."

The animal's hooves were dirty and needed to be trimmed. There were burs caught in her mane and tail and the drainage around one of her eyes was most likely equine conjunctivitis. "When was the last time Ruby was seen by a vet?"

Melissa nodded her head toward the barn doors, indicating she'd rather speak to him in private.

"Go ahead, Logan," Sadie said. "The boys and I will wait with Ruby."

Logan followed Melissa to the front of the barn, where they stopped out of earshot of Sadie and the twins. "I'm estranged from my father." Melissa dug the toe of her boot in the dirt. The young woman couldn't be more than twenty-five. "I haven't seen him in over twelve years. I wouldn't be here now if his neighbor hadn't phoned and told me that he'd had a stroke."

"I'm sorry."

She shrugged off his condolences. "He's in an assisted living home, but as you can see he's let this place go. His neighbor came over every few days to make sure the animals were fed, but other than that they've been neglected."

"Are there more animals on the property?"

"I found homes for the dogs, cats, chickens and the mule." She rubbed her brow. "I contacted a local rescue group, but they've got more horses than the volunteers can keep up with. They asked me to try to find Ruby a home."

"Do you have any idea where your father bought the horse?"

"The neighbor says he got her from a carnival that came through the area years ago."

Until a vet examined the animal, Logan wouldn't know if she could be used for rides.

"I'd offer to pay a vet to take care of her eye infection and trim her hooves," Melissa said, "but I don't have the money."

Logan glanced across the barn. Tyler was petting Ruby's nose. Tommy was crouched down pushing the hay on the floor into tiny piles by his feet. Sadie studied the horse, her brow furrowed and mouth pinched—she was worried about the animal, too.

"You can have her for free. And you're welcome to take whatever feed or tack is in the shed. Everything on the property will be auctioned off in two weeks."

Logan watched the gentle way Tyler patted Ruby's head and then leaned down and whispered something in her ear. The kid had a huge heart. Logan had no idea if he'd be able to use Ruby in the petting zoo, but how could he leave her behind? "Let's load her in the trailer."

"Thank you so much," Melissa said. "I'll check the shed for feed."

"Leave it. We've got plenty at our place." He didn't want to risk feeding the animal food that might be contaminated.

Melissa glanced at her watch. "I have an appointment with the convalescent home in twenty minutes. Do you need help getting Ruby into the trailer?"

"I can manage, thanks."

Melissa stuck out her hand. "Thanks again. I can tell she'll be in good hands and your sons will treat her kindly."

Sons. The word echoed in Logan's head as he watched Melissa get into her car and drive off. More than a few times in the past week he'd thought about what it would be like to be the twins' father. His chest felt heavy when he thought of waiting a year, maybe two, before Sadie and the boys returned to Stampede for another visit.

He walked back to the trio. "Looks like Ruby will have a new home at Paradise Ranch."

Sadie sent him a relieved look. "Is she healthy enough to travel?"

"She'll be fine. I'll ask the vet to come out today or tomorrow and look her over."

Tommy kicked the piles of straw he'd gathered and tiny clouds of dust rose from the ground. "How come we gotta get another girl horse, Uncle Logan?"

"You might not like girls now," he said, "but you'll think they're pretty cool when you're older."

"Yuck." Tommy wrinkled his nose.

"What did you pay for Ruby?" Sadie asked.

"She was free." Logan grasped her arm and pulled her away from the kids. "I don't know if we'll be able to use her in the petting zoo. It all depends on how old and sick she is."

"Then why are you taking her?" she asked.

Logan glanced at Tyler, who continued his one-sided conversation with the pony. "Tyler may have found his first best friend."

Sadie stood on her tiptoes and kissed his cheek. "You have a big heart, Uncle Logan."

If only Sadie would give him a chance, she'd find out exactly how big his heart was. "Let's take Ruby home, boys."

Home. The word had just slipped out, but it was true. Paradise Ranch had never felt more like home than it had since Sadie and her sons arrived in Stampede.

An hour and a half later Logan pulled up to the corral at the ranch and the twins piled out of the back seat. "Time to give Ruby a bath." He nudged Sadie and smiled. "You should help, too."

She shook her head. "I need to work on a budget. You boys are on your own."

"I left notes on the desk in the office for you," he said.

"What kind of notes?"

"Information that might help when you speak to contractors."

"That was nice of you. Thanks."

He hoped the lists would impress Sadie. Focusing on the task hadn't been easy when a hundred other things had popped into his mind, so he'd swallowed his pride and asked his grandfather for help. Together they'd jotted down everything that needed to be done to get the project off the ground. And the longer they'd chatted, the more animated his grandfather had grown. As much as the old man professed to hate the idea of adding a tourist attraction to the ranch, he was determined to make sure it was a success. And when he'd left the office that night, there had been more pep in his step.

For so long Logan had tried to handle everything on his own. Discovering that it was easier to focus and keep track of his thoughts when he was working with someone was an eye-opener.

"Boys, listen to Uncle Logan," Sadie said. "And no goofing off around Ruby."

"Okay!" they answered.

Sadie snagged Logan's shirtsleeve. "If the boys don't do as you say, threaten them with an early bedtime."

"They'll be fine." He waited for her to walk off, but she kept staring at him.

Her gaze clung to his, her baby blues sparkling. "Thank you."

"For what?" he asked.

"Just for being you."

He stared at her retreating back, his heart doubling in size. "Before we give Ruby a bath, we need to remove the burs in her tail and mane."

"What's a bur?" Tommy asked, following Logan into the barn. Tyler brought up the rear.

"A bur is a pricker." Logan pulled on a pair of work gloves.

"What's a pricker?" Tyler asked.

"I'll show you." They walked over to the corral, where he'd put Ruby after he'd unloaded her from the trailer. Logan hoisted Tommy onto the top rail, then sat Tyler next to him. "I'll remove the burs and you two watch. That way you won't get your finger stuck by one." He pulled out the first bur and showed the kids.

"Can I touch it?" Tommy asked.

The boy was a daredevil for sure. "Nope."

"What are we gonna do after you get the burs out?" Tommy asked.

"Hose Ruby off and then scrub her with horse soap." Logan worked on Ruby's tail and then her mane. After ten minutes he said, "I think she's ready for a bath. Let's get the supplies." He set the kids on the ground and they returned to the barn.

"Tommy, take the shampoo." Logan handed him a half gallon of livestock soap and he wrapped both arms around the bottle. "Tyler, you carry the bucket with the grooming tools." Logan picked up the hose and a handful of towels and they returned to the corral.

Logan attached the hose to the spigot on the side of

the barn. "Now we give Ruby something to eat so she's happy while she's getting her bath." Logan moved the feeder in the pen closer to the horse. While she ate grain, he turned on the hose and motioned for Tyler and Tommy to stand next to him. "Don't spray her face." He let the boys take turns wetting down Ruby. Then he dribbled shampoo over her hide and handed soft-bristled brushes to the boys. "Start scrubbing. Nice and easy. Don't push too hard."

Logan paid attention to Ruby's body language, ready to intervene if her muscles tensed, but she loved the bath, closing her eyes between mouthfuls of grain. "I think we're through. You guys were a big help." He lifted the boys onto the rail and then rinsed the horse.

"Ruby's got big teeth," Tommy said.

Tyler pointed at the horse's muzzle. "And she's got hair in her nose."

Logan chuckled. "That's because Ruby's an old lady."

"Like Aunt Amelia?"

"Just like Aunt Amelia." Logan trained the hose on Ruby's legs, then the ground around the horse's hooves until it turned to mud.

"How come you're getting her feet dirty?" Tyler asked.

"The mud will soften Ruby's nails and make it easier for the vet to trim her hooves."

While Ruby's feet soaked in mud, Logan took a damp rag and gently wiped the mare's face, noticing that her eyes appeared cloudy. If she couldn't see well, she might be frightened around a large group of kids. Time would tell if they could use her in the petting zoo.

"Uncle Logan," Tyler said, "I wish you were my dad."

Tommy's head snapped in his brother's direction, then he looked at Logan, waiting for him to respond.

"That means a lot, Tyler. I'm glad you like me."

"I like you, too," Tommy said.

Logan grinned. "I've enjoyed having you boys here at the ranch."

He rinsed the rag while the brothers whispered in each other's ears. When they broke apart, Tommy asked, "Do you want to be our dad?"

The lump that formed in Logan's throat made it impossible to answer. He swallowed twice, then said, "I'm already your uncle."

"You can be our dad, too," Tyler said.

Logan took a deep breath. How was he supposed to handle this? He stared at the house, wishing Sadie would walk outside and rescue him.

"Our dad doesn't like us," Tyler said.

Surprised by the boy's confession, Logan tried to reassure the pair. "Your father loves you guys."

They shook their heads, their little faces sober. "Our dad moved to Balkimore," Tommy said.

"When dads move away, it doesn't mean they stop loving you." As soon as the words left his mouth, Logan realized how hollow they sounded. He remembered the feeling of having a parent walk out of his life—it felt like crap.

"Our dad hates soccer," Tyler said. "And he yells at Tommy 'cause he can't sit still."

"You don't yell at me." Tommy stared at Logan.

Jeez. How had these two pint-size hooligans wrapped their fingers around his heart so quickly? "I'm honored that you boys want me to be your father, but—"

"Mom!" Tommy ducked between the rails, then raced across the yard, Tyler following his brother. The boys stopped in front of Sadie, both talking at once, their arms gesturing wildly. Logan couldn't hear a word they said, but when Sadie's mouth dropped open, he had a pretty good idea.

Sadie took Tommy and Tyler by the hands and walked them back to the corral. Logan stayed where he was, half hidden behind Ruby. He was out of his comfort zone and more than happy to let Sadie take the lead in this situation.

"I didn't know my boys were interviewing for fathers."

Logan kept his mouth shut.

"Can Uncle Logan be our dad?" Tyler asked.

"Uncle Logan is already your uncle," Sadie said.

Tommy climbed the corral rail and peered over Ruby's back at Logan. "Can uncles be dads, too?"

Logan glanced at Sadie and the warm expression on her face confused the heck out of him. "I reckon some uncles are fathers, too."

"See, Mom," Tommy said. "He can be our uncle and our dad."

"You guys go up to the house and help Gramps. He's making cookies in the kitchen."

The boys took off and Logan chuckled. "Hard to keep good help these days."

Sadie climbed the rails, then dropped down into the corral. "Tell me what to do."

He walked Ruby away from the muddy ground, then motioned to the hose. "You can rinse her hooves off now." They worked in silence for several minutes.

"She seems like a gentle horse," Sadie said.

"After the vet checks her eyes and the infection clears up, we'll know whether or not she can be used for pony rides."

"I'm sorry the boys put you on the spot like that."

Logan smiled. "I think they put you on the spot more than me."

"What do you mean?"

He shrugged. "I've wondered what it would be like to be their father."

Her eyes widened and Logan's gut clenched. Had he gone too far? Was it too soon? He bent over and felt a blast of water hit his back.

Sadie blinked her innocent eyes. "I'm sorry. I wasn't paying attention."

He bent over again to dry Ruby's hoof. This time the water hit the back of his head. Keeping a straight face, he turned around and said, "Maybe you need help figuring out how to use that hose."

"You don't think I know how to handle a hose?" She sprayed his chest until she'd soaked his shirt.

"We're playing games, are we?" He walked toward Sadie and she backpedaled, blasting him in the face with water. Half blinded, he kept coming and didn't stop until he'd backed her up against the rails and the hose was smashed between their bodies. Then he leaned in and kissed her—not a sweet, innocent peck on the lips but a kiss that told her how much he wanted her. When they came up for air, he peeled a lock of wet hair off her cheek. "Has a cowboy ever invited you up to his hayloft before?"

Sadie stared at Logan's mouth and she shook her head.

He turned off the hose and dropped it to the ground, then took Sadie's hand and escorted her into the barn.

"We don't have much time," she said, giggling. "Baking cookies with your grandfather won't keep the boys busy for long."

He motioned for Sadie to climb the ladder first and then he followed her up, his gaze riveted to her sashaying fanny inches from his face. When they reached the loft, he pulled her into his arms. "I'll show you how much we can accomplish in a half hour."

When Logan whisked Sadie's shirt over her head, she shushed the voices in her brain cautioning her. Now wasn't the time to overthink the moment…to wonder if what they were doing was smart…to try to make sense of where this would lead them…

She pressed herself against Logan, grateful for the shadows in the loft that hid her blushing cheeks. When she fumbled with the buttons on his Western shirt, Logan grew impatient. He stepped back and Sadie helped him peel the wet material over his shoulders and down his arms. Another tug-of-war commenced as they helped each other out of their wet jeans. After five minutes they were both breathing hard.

Logan pulled her naked body against his and their laughter faded.

"You're beautiful, Sadie," he whispered before kissing her.

She squirmed against him when his hands explored her. Call her crazy but Logan made her feel young and foolish and even a little bit in love. In his arms she forgot about the future. She felt safe, cherished and content.

When he ended the kiss, she whispered, "So how does this work?"

He pressed his lower body against hers and she laughed. "I meant are we doing this dance standing up or lying down?"

He peered over the edge of the loft. "Wait here."

Like she had a choice, being buck naked? He shimmied down the ladder and she heard a door open and then close. A few seconds later he returned with a blanket.

She took his hand and led him into the shadows in the corner and he spread the blanket over the bales of hay.

"I'm on the pill." She sucked in a quick breath. "I'm sorry. I wasn't thinking."

He brushed his knuckles across her cheek. "It's okay. And just so you know, I always use a condom." He reached for the wallet in his jeans pocket, then he kissed Sadie and they lost themselves in a tangle of arms and legs.

Chapter Twelve

Logan trailed his fingers down Sadie's naked back, over her hip and across her thigh. He closed his eyes and willed the world to stop moving for a few short minutes—long enough to savor the feeling of rightness seeping into his bones.

"Can I say something, or—" Sadie wiggled her leg between his "—do you have a no-talking policy after sex?"

He winced at her choice of words. *Sex* sounded cold and empty—the opposite of how he felt right now. "I don't mind talking."

She pressed her mouth against his chest and he snuggled her closer. "This complicates things." She propped herself up on her elbow and rubbed her finger across his lower lip. "Acting normal around you now is going to be difficult."

He tucked a strand of hair behind her ear. Why had he never noticed her petite earlobes or her slender, regal neck? She was a capable, strong woman, but when she was lying naked on top of him, she felt delicate and vulnerable and he wanted to protect her from everything bad in the world. "You're a special woman," he said. "Nothing fazes you. No matter what roadblock you face, you keep moving forward, stronger than before."

She nuzzled her nose against his cheek, and he swallowed hard. In the short time they'd been together he was having difficulty envisioning a future that didn't involve being a part of her and the boys' everyday lives.

"I wish I could say it was easy being a single mom, but there have been days where nothing goes right and everything goes wrong. I manage because I don't have a choice. There's no one else to help pick up the slack." She exhaled, her breath cooling off Logan's skin. "How do you do it? The boys aren't even your sons, but the three of you are comfortable around one another."

"I see a lot of myself in Tommy. Watching him interact with Tyler has helped me understand what it must have been like for my brothers when we were younger. I was the one who created havoc in the family and my parents and grandparents spent all their time and energy reining me in while Gunner and Reid got overlooked."

"May I ask you a personal question?"

He forced his muscles to relax, but his pulse sped up. "Sure."

"Where did you and Beth meet?"

"We met in a bar after a rodeo in Oklahoma. We hit it off and traveled the circuit together. She was a decent barrel racer, but a bulging disc in her lower back kept her sidelined on and off during her career. She was considering retiring from the circuit. Then I got the call to come home and manage the ranch and Beth decided it was a sign for her to quit rodeo. We were in Nevada at the time, so we stopped at a wedding chapel and got married."

"Talk about whirlwind."

"Reality sank in a few months after we'd arrived at the ranch and Beth got to know the real me."

"What do you mean the real you?"

"The Logan who can't focus." He braved a smile even though the memory still stung. "She was used to being with the Logan who made riding bulls look easy. She couldn't understand how she'd send me to the store for milk and I'd come home with everything but milk."

"It must have gotten more stressful when you tried to start a family."

"She gave it nine months before setting up doctor's appointments for both of us." Logan would never forget the look on Beth's face when the doctor told them Logan was sterile. Tears had poured down her pale cheeks. She'd opened her mouth over and over to speak, but she couldn't find her voice. She'd been devastated.

"I'm sorry."

"Getting divorced was the right decision. Beth's happy now. She remarried and has a couple of kids."

"Do you keep in touch with her?"

"No. I took Gramps to a doctor's appointment last year in San Antonio. Beth's parents are from there, and she and her kids were visiting them when we ran into each other at the Cracker Barrel. Gramps loves that restaurant."

Logan cuddled Sadie closer and ignored the panic rising in him. There was no doubt in his mind that she believed he was good with the twins and that he cared for the boys as if they were his own. And he wanted to believe she'd recognized a deeper connection with him after they'd made love. But he still felt she was holding a part of herself back from him. He understood she wanted another child someday, but she'd never said she wasn't open to adoption or the use of a sperm donor. He believed Sadie's hesitation was because of his ADD. He thought back to the doctor's appointment this past March and the suggestion that he give cognitive behavioral therapy a try. If he wanted a chance to be a part of Sadie and the twins' lives, and to prove to her that she could count on him to follow through, he needed to show her that he was taking steps to better manage his ADD. If he could show that he was an asset to her and not a liability, then maybe she'd stay in Texas and not return to Wisconsin.

Sadie wiggled free. "We'd better check on the boys before they come looking for us." Between laughter and heated gazes they managed to pull on their damp clothes and make themselves presentable.

When they reached the back porch, the smell of baking cookies drifted through the screen door. Logan followed Sadie into the kitchen, then pulled up short. A flour bomb had exploded in the room. Tommy and Tyler stood on chairs next to the counter, taking turns rolling out dough. Emmett removed a batch of cookies from the oven and set the baking sheet on the stove, then turned around. His eyes widened. "You got hay in your hair." His gaze switched to Logan. "And you got hay sticking out of places it shouldn't be."

"If you'll excuse me, I'm going to clean up." Sadie escaped the room, and when her footsteps echoed on the stairs, Logan looked back at his grandfather. They both struggled to control their twitching lips.

"'Bout time you made a move on that gal," Gramps said.

Logan ignored him.

Gramps nodded. "Doc Landers called. He finished his last appointment early and said he'd be here before the end of the day to look at Ruby."

"Good deal."

"Logan?"

"What?"

Emmett's gaze swung to the ceiling when the sound of running water whooshed through the walls. "Nothing."

"Behave, guys."

"We will," the boys echoed in unison.

"Where you going?" Gramps asked.

"To run an errand."

"Aren't you changing first?" He eyed Logan's wet clothes.

"I'll drive with the windows down."

Logan hopped into his pickup. He opened the glove compartment and removed the business card he'd held on to all these months, then he input the address of the doctor's office into the GPS app on his phone.

A half hour later, Logan parked in front of a Victorian home on Main Street in Mesquite. It was one of several historic houses in town that had been converted into business offices. "Brian Hofstadter, MD, CBT" was painted in white letters across the glass pane on the front door.

Before he lost his courage, he left the pickup and

climbed the porch steps. When he entered the house, a young woman looked up from the desk in the foyer.

"May I help you?"

"I'd like to schedule an appointment with Dr. Hofstadter."

"Have you seen the doctor before?" she asked.

"I'm a new patient." Logan could have just as easily called the office to schedule the appointment, but he hoped that by showing up in person and completing the paperwork in advance he wouldn't chicken out and cancel the meeting at the last minute.

"Do you have insurance?" she asked.

He set his card on the desk and she handed him a clipboard. "Please fill out these forms and then we'll set up your appointment."

The paperwork took ten minutes to complete and a short while later Logan walked out of the office with an appointment card for the following Monday at three in the afternoon. He had no idea if the therapy would help, but he hoped Sadie would give him credit for trying. When he returned to town, he stopped at Amelia's house.

The old woman's eyes looked past him when she opened the front door. "Where are Sadie and the boys?"

"At the ranch." He removed his hat. "Do you have a moment to talk?"

"Come in." She stepped back, then closed the door behind him.

"I think this is the first time I've been inside your home."

"Really?" Amelia signaled him to follow her into the kitchen. He made himself comfortable at the table and watched her pour him a glass of iced tea before taking the seat across from him. "What brings you by?"

"I wanted to thank you for making things right with the bank on Gramps's and my behalf." He gulped the tea.

"Did Emmett tell you that we talked last night?"

Logan shook his head.

"He called at two in the morning." Amelia's eyebrow arched. "Fortunately when you get to be our age you're usually awake at that hour."

"He didn't start an argument, did he?"

"On the contrary. He apologized for being an ass—his word, not mine." She smiled.

"That's why I stopped by. Don't let my grandfather fool you into believing he's upset that you paid the bank off. I think he likes the idea of getting up in the mornings now and having something to do."

"Emmett hasn't been himself since your grandmother died. The only time he leaves the property is to meet with the town council or hunt me down to argue." She sighed. "I hope you're right and that the activity at the ranch will keep him too busy to be grumpy."

If Amelia was worried about his grandfather, Logan knew her heart was in the right place.

"I have an ulterior motive for wanting this tourist attraction to succeed."

Uh-oh. "What's that?" he asked.

"I want Sadie and the twins to remain in Stampede indefinitely."

Logan's heart skipped a beat.

"I'd like to offer Sadie a permanent job keeping the books for the business once it's up and running." She held up a hand. "With your and Emmett's permission. I'd pay her salary, of course."

His heart beat faster when he thought of Amelia becoming an ally in his plan to convince Sadie to stay in Stampede. "And if Sadie declines your offer?"

"Then I'll pay someone else to keep the books. You and Emmett will be too busy taking care of the animals and tourists." Amelia smiled. "I assume you and Emmett will be on board with my plan?"

Logan nodded. "I'm sure it's obvious that I care for Sadie and the twins. And Gramps loves having the boys around."

"Between the two of us," Amelia said, "we should be able to convince my niece to make Stampede her new home."

Logan pushed his chair back and stood. Now more than ever he was determined to follow through with his appointment with Dr. Hofstadter and prove that he was serious about being a man Sadie could depend on.

"I gave Sadie the green light to spruce up the entire property." Her eyes twinkled. "If things get too crazy for Emmett, you tell him he has an open invitation to stay in town with me." She tapped her finger against the table. "You know…if your grandfather really objected to my interference, he could have stopped me long ago."

But Gramps hadn't. The old man had grumbled and complained about Amelia butting into his business, but he was allowing her to get away with it. *Because he likes the attention.*

Logan grabbed his hat and Amelia walked him to the front door. "Mind if I offer a little advice, Ms. Amelia?"

Her eyes narrowed.

"You two might save yourselves a whole lot of aggravation if you'd just kiss and make up."

"WHERE'S LOGAN?" EMMETT stopped in the doorway of the office and stared at Sadie.

"I don't know." She glanced at the new clock radio sitting on the desk. "He drove off a couple of hours ago." She wasn't sure why Logan had bought the desk clock when there was a perfectly good clock hanging on the wall above the sofa.

"That's the second time this week he's taken off without telling me."

Sadie wondered what Logan had done to get himself in the doghouse with his grandfather. "He probably got called away to check on something."

Emmett's mouth twisted into a frown. Okay, so she was making excuses for Logan, but she wanted to defend him. The past week he'd been so conscientious that she'd almost forgotten her concerns about his ADD. Every night before she left the ranch, he'd come into the office and they'd discussed plans for the next day. He'd purchased a journal to write down calls he needed to make and other tasks she asked him to do. And after they finished talking business, he'd close the office door, take her hand and kiss her. Sometimes he led her to the couch, where they did more than kiss, and other times he held her in his arms and they danced to a song playing on the radio.

"Maybe I can help with something," she said.

A loud racket distracted Emmett and she followed him out of the room and onto the front porch. Two dump trucks, filled with gravel, and a grader drove toward the house. "Aunt Amelia gave the go-ahead to lay down new gravel and fix the potholes in the driveway." Sadie didn't know what made her happier, not having to swerve around the craters after today or knowing Logan had followed through and arranged for the work to be done sooner than she'd asked. When Emmett scowled, she said, "We can't have people blowing a tire before they reach the petting zoo."

"That woman's got too much money to spend." He opened the door. "I promised the boys they could play in the tree house. We'll be out there if you need me."

"Don't forget to take the walkie-talkies." She'd purchased the electronics for Emmett and the twins so she'd know where they were when she was working in the office. "They're on the table in the hallway." Next to another new clock that had appeared out of the blue one day last week.

A cloud of dust billowed in the distance—Logan's pickup. He parked by her van, then waved before he walked over to speak with the construction workers. After a few minutes he climbed the porch steps wearing a huge smile. "You're in a good mood," she said.

"I just got off the phone with Smith Painting and Drywall in San Antonio."

Lydia had used the company to paint the motel and was pleased with their work, so Sadie had asked Logan to follow up with the company.

"The owner, Brett Smith, will be here tomorrow to give us an estimate on the barn and the house."

"That's great. Thanks." When Sadie had agreed to temporarily stay on as the bookkeeper/business manager at the ranch while she waited to hear whether or not the special preschool would accept Tommy, she'd prepared herself for a challenging, stressful assignment. She hadn't thought she could count on Logan to do his part, but he was following through on every task, making her job a breeze.

He pulled the leather planner from his pocket. "Remember when you and I were tossing ideas around about public bathrooms for guests?"

"I do."

"The guy who runs the feed store in Mesquite gave me the number of a company that specializes in building outhouses that use a vacuum system to dispose of waste." He pulled a sticky notepad out of his front pocket and wrote down the man's name and phone number. "He said to give him a call. He's got one set up in his backyard if you want to see what it looks like."

"Thanks, I'll contact him." She laughed.

"What's so funny?"

"You're Mr. All Business lately."

"Come with me." She followed him into the house. He closed the front door, then backed her up against the wall, bracing his hands on either side of her head. "I've been thinking about kissing you since I woke up this morning."

She played with the snaps on his shirt, unable to concentrate with his lips on her mouth. This wasn't supposed to happen. She couldn't be falling more in love with Logan, but how could she stop herself when each day she looked forward to working with him on the ranch projects and could hardly wait until their end-of-evening meetings in the office? Logan was proving to be a worthy partner.

"Will you meet me at the Moonlight Motel tonight?" he asked.

"What time?"

He lifted his head, and when he gazed into her eyes, she swore there were tiny sparks of light flashing in their dark depths. "Will the boys be in bed by ten?"

"Yes." She'd make sure her aunt knew where to find her if the twins needed anything in the middle of the night.

Logan gave her a quick kiss, then ducked out of the house. She returned to the office, where she struggled to focus on the estimates she'd received for the construction of a new horse barn. What was going on? Everything was upside down and inside out this week. Logan should be the one struggling to stay organized, not her.

She jotted down *Logan…Motel…10 p.m.* on her to-do list—then added two exclamation points and a smiley face.

LOGAN PULLED SADIE close and adjusted the blankets over them. Gunner had given him the key card to the San Antonio room at the Moonlight Motel and it hadn't taken them long to get naked. "Does your aunt know where you are?" he asked.

"Yes, and so does your grandfather."

"What?"

"Emmett showed up at the house insisting he and my aunt needed to clear the air."

"Clear the air about what?"

"I don't know. Aunt Amelia sent him up to the attic to play with the boys, and he stayed up there until I called them down for their baths. Then your grandfather insisted on reading them a bedtime story, which turned into three stories, and it was nine thirty when I turned out the lights."

"Did Gramps leave after that?"

"Nope. He and Aunt Amelia were sitting on the front porch in the rocking chairs when I left for the motel."

Logan smiled. "Maybe he'll kiss her tonight."

She drew circles on his chest, distracting him.

Logan repeated the simple mantra Dr. Hofstadter had come up with for him in their first session.

I'm the boss of my thoughts.

When Logan's attention drifted, he repeated the mantra in his head. At first it had done nothing to help. But he'd continued to practice saying the phrase, and just the past couple of days he was able to recall his last thought before he'd become distracted.

I'm the boss of my thoughts. "You called me Mr. All Business this afternoon."

Her finger stopped moving. "I meant it as a compliment," she said. "You've been a huge help to me in getting this project off the ground."

He tightened his arms around her. "I've been seeing a doctor in Mesquite who specializes in cognitive behavioral therapy."

Sadie lifted her head and stared into his eyes. "Is that why there are clocks everywhere in the house?"

He raised his left arm in the air. "I started wearing a watch, too."

"And the pocket planner you carry around?"

"I write everything down. Whatever pops into my mind that isn't in the planner, I tell myself it doesn't exist, and it helps me focus on what I'm doing at that moment." And it decreased his stress. "The doctor says if I keep at it, my ability to stay focused will grow stronger and I might not need the journal anymore."

"I'm happy for you." Sadie rested her head against his chest and Logan swept his fingers over her bare back.

The doctor had been impressed with his improvement when they'd reviewed his home therapy lessons. Logan hoped that if he continued to make progress Sadie would be more than just happy for him—she'd be happy for her, too.

"I may need to look into that kind of therapy if Tommy doesn't get into the special preschool he's on a waiting list for."

"What special school?"

"The name's kind of cute," she said. "It's called Busy Little Minds Preschool. It's for kids with ADD. I'm crossing my fingers that Tommy gets in next semester." Logan pulled in a deep breath and exhaled slowly. It sounded like she'd already made up her mind to leave Texas.

"The school's not cheap, but if it helps Tommy, he'll have a better chance of being successful in kindergarten and I won't have to worry about him being held back a year."

"The therapist I'm seeing only works with adults, but he may know of someone who specializes in helping children." If Tommy started therapy, that would mean Sadie would have to commit to staying in Stampede or somewhere nearby, which was exactly what he wanted her to do.

Her fingers trailed over Logan's stomach and down his thigh.

I'm the boss of my thoughts. His mantra reminded him that he hadn't asked Sadie to meet him at the motel to discuss behavioral therapy techniques. He rolled her beneath him and, with single-minded determination, showed her just how much he needed her—all of her.

Chapter Thirteen

"Look, Mom!" Tommy pointed out the window of the van.

A trio of pickups sat parked in the ranch yard, and two men stood on ladders spraying red paint across the side of the barn. "I see," she said. "The barn looks great."

A month had passed since Sadie and Logan had rendezvoused at the Moonlight Motel. It was the third week in October, and work on the property had shifted into high gear, sending her and Logan in opposite directions during the day. At suppertime, they joined the twins and Emmett in the kitchen along with Amelia. Sadie's aunt had begun showing up in the afternoons with one excuse or another about needing to speak with Emmett, and she'd stick around long enough for Emmett to invite her to join the family for supper. Amelia's presence in the house was noticeable everywhere. The pile of Western shirts Sadie had seen sitting on the ironing board weeks earlier had vanished and the smell of lemon furniture polish lingered in the air.

Each night after dinner, Sadie and her aunt would clean up the kitchen while the men took the boys to the barn and visited the horses. Later, the family would gather on the front porch, Emmett and Amelia sitting side by side on the swing regaling the twins with stories of their childhood in Stampede.

"Can we paint, too?" Tommy asked.

"No, honey. You can't help paint the barn."

Life was good—better than good. The biggest change Sadie had seen in herself since arriving in Stampede was a decrease in her stress level. She was busy every day, but life wasn't chaotic. She and Logan had settled into a routine that included meeting over coffee in the morning to discuss any last-minute changes to their to-do lists. And at the end of the day she looked forward to Logan's kiss goodbye before she left the ranch with the boys and her aunt.

Never had Sadie imagined that taking a break from life would lead to this feeling of contentment. And Logan was a huge reason for her and the boys' happiness.

"Can we ride Ruby?" Tyler asked.

"You'll have to ask Logan." Poor Logan fielded a million questions a day about Ruby and the other horses, and he answered every one of them without growing frustrated.

In order to show she supported Logan's efforts to get a handle on his ADD, she made sure the tasks she assigned him didn't interfere with his therapy sessions. After making great strides in such a short time, the doctor had recommended that Logan attend only one session a week instead of two. No one in the family had remarked on the changes in him, but Sadie saw them.

When Logan talked to his grandfather, he no longer curled his fingers into the palms of his hands. And when he came into the office and they chatted about the various projects under construction, his gaze didn't wander around the room—it stayed on her.

Each night when she drove away with the boys, the tiny ache in her chest lasted a little longer before it faded. Then at bedtime when she closed her eyes, she envisioned a future for her and her sons. A future she couldn't imagine without Logan in it.

Then last week the Busy Little Minds Preschool had called Sadie to inform her that Tommy had been accepted into their spring program. She should have been ecstatic, but when she thought about leaving Stampede, she wanted to cry. She couldn't say for sure why she hadn't told anyone the news—maybe because she hoped for some sort of sign telling her that it was the best place for Tommy to be.

"Look at the rosebushes, boys." She parked by the front porch. The TLC she'd showered on the Knock Out roses had finally paid off. The bushes were in full bloom—an advantage to living in the south, where shrubs and flowers blossomed well into the fall.

"Can we go see Gramps?" Tyler pointed to where Emmett sat in a lawn chair observing the work crew.

"Make sure you stay with Gramps and don't go near the barn, where the men are working. Understood?" She glanced in the rearview mirror and watched their heads nod in unison. She hit the button on the key fob that opened the back door, and the boys crawled out of their booster seats, then jumped to the ground and raced across the yard. Sadie was halfway up the porch steps when her cell phone went off. It was a 608 area code—Madison. "Hello?"

The caller on the other end was a headhunter wanting to schedule an interview with Sadie for a job that had opened up at a dentist's office in the suburb of Middleton. Sadie's former boss had passed along her name to the dental practice searching for a new office manager. The position sounded too good to be true—a $10,000 jump in salary would cover the cost of Tommy's new preschool. Was this the sign she'd been waiting for?

She swallowed twice before she found her voice. "How soon would you need me to come in for an interview?" Her mouth dropped open. "I'm afraid I can't make it tomorrow. I'm actually in Texas right now visiting family." The woman offered to reschedule for Friday afternoon, then ended the call.

Sadie sat on the porch swing. Agreeing to the interview had been a gut reaction to the call. Or had it? She stared down the gravel driveway. After Aunt Amelia had asked her to consider staying on as the ranch bookkeeper once the riding trail and petting zoo opened to the public, Sadie had allowed herself to pretend Stampede was her and the boys' new home. And then there was Logan. He was showing her every day, in so many ways, that they were good together. And no one could question his love for her sons. They were becoming the perfect family in every way but one.

She'd been an idiot for believing he'd only bring more disorder to her and the boys' lives. She understood that once he completed his therapy sessions, his ADD wouldn't magically disappear. His difficulty focusing would be with him his entire life, but so would his desire and determination to manage it.

She drew in a steadying breath. Logan was working

hard to get a handle on his ADD because he loved her and the boys. Maybe he hadn't said the words yet, but his eyes had. His love for them was in his gaze every time he looked at her or smiled at her sons. Now the job offer made it impossible for Sadie to use the high tuition of the new preschool as an excuse for staying in Stampede. The job interview reminded her that Tommy was her number one priority. With the right help, he might be able to avoid the troubles Logan had experienced growing up. She wanted Tommy to look back on his childhood knowing his mother had done everything within her power to help him even if it meant sacrificing her own happiness.

Sadie's phone rang, only this time it was Scarlett. "What are you up to?"

"Not much. I have a quick break between clients and wanted to catch up with you. See how the twins are doing."

"The boys are great…but speaking of Madison, I got a call from a headhunter about a job in Middleton."

"You don't sound excited."

"I'm not."

Scarlett groaned. "Don't tell me you're going to follow in Lydia's footsteps and stay in Stampede?"

"I'm tempted. The boys have never been happier. Tyler doesn't read anymore to escape from his brother's hyperactivity. He's come out of his shell and yesterday he didn't even pick up a book to read."

"He quit reading?"

"He reads at bedtime and Tommy sits with him and listens to the story."

"That's great."

"Logan's grandfather takes the boys fishing all the

time, and at the end of the day we have supper together with Aunt Amelia, and then the boys help Logan and Emmett take care of the horses and Ruby."

"Who's Ruby?"

"A miniature horse we picked up for the petting zoo. She's the sweetest thing." Sadie laughed. "The other day Tommy asked if Ruby could play in the tree house Logan built for them."

"Logan built a tree house?"

"There's so much for the boys to do at the ranch. And when it rains, the kids have fun playing at Aunt Amelia's in the attic."

"Sadie?"

"What?"

"Do the twins miss Pete?" Scarlett asked.

"If they do, they haven't told me."

"Lydia said you and Logan are getting along well. Is he part of the reason you're hesitant to come home?"

"Yes." But also Madison didn't feel like home anymore—Stampede did.

"You fell in love with Logan, didn't you?"

Sadie closed her eyes and tried to imagine leaving the ranch and Logan behind—she couldn't. "I think I did," she whispered.

"Do they put something in the water in Stampede? First Lydia goes down there and ends up pregnant by Gunner and then sneaks off to Vegas to get married. Then you visit and fall in love with Logan." Scarlett gasped. "Are you pregnant?"

"Of course not." A tiny ache squeezed Sadie's heart, but the pain dissipated quickly.

"What about the interview for the job in Middleton? Are you coming back for it?"

"Yes. I'm flying up. The interview is on Friday."

"I think it's a great backup plan," Scarlett said.

"Backup plan?"

"For when you ask Logan what his intentions are toward you and the boys. If he doesn't have forever in mind, you'll have a job waiting for you in Madison."

Sadie was caught between choosing what was best for her and what was best for her son. Walking away from Logan would be one of the hardest things she'd ever have to do. The memory of watching him give the boys rides in the wheelbarrow flashed before her eyes. He'd embraced her sons from the moment he'd met them.

She changed the subject. "Aunt Amelia wants to know when you're coming down here for a visit."

"Maybe in the spring when Lydia has the baby."

"She's having an ultrasound next week. Her doctor believes the due date she was given at her first appointment was wrong."

"When does she think she's due?"

"Possibly the beginning of March."

"One of you let me know when you find out so I can put in a request for vacation."

"We will."

"Got another call coming in. Let me know when to pick you up at the airport."

"Thanks, Scarlett. I love you."

"Love you, too!"

Sadie ended the call and went into the house. She set her purse on the office desk before walking through the kitchen and out the back door. There, she stopped and took in the scene before her.

The side of the barn facing the house sported a

fresh coat of red paint and bright white trim. Emmett sat in a lawn chair tossing chicken feed to a strange-looking bird with a huge feather bouffant on top of its head—probably a new addition to the petting zoo. Inside the corral, Logan was walking Ruby in circles while she towed the boys in the Radio Flyer wagon. The horse's eye infection had cleared up and she'd gained weight since coming to the ranch. The vet had vaccinated her and pronounced her strong enough to be used for pony rides in the petting zoo.

Tommy and Tyler wore the miniature cowboy hats their aunt Lydia had bought for them, insisting when they woke up this morning that they wanted to be cowboys just like Uncle Logan. The horse's tail swished in front of Tommy's face, and each time he captured the tail, Ruby tugged it free and he laughed. Tyler leaned over the side of the wagon and plucked the head off a dandelion and dropped it down the back of Tommy's shirt.

Tears burned Sadie's eyes and she could barely catch her breath—it was as if someone had stepped on her chest. Her gaze swung to Logan. He was grinning from ear to ear, having as much fun as the twins. Sadie checked the time on her phone—Logan needed to drive into Mesquite for his therapy session. But instead of grabbing a bite to eat or taking a few moments to relax before he left, he was playing with her sons.

Her gaze skipped around the yard. She'd lived her entire adult life in apartments, cooped up in a few rooms. She'd had to get into the car and take the boys to a park if they'd wanted to play outside and run around. The ranch was a hundred times better than any playground, and it was right outside the back door.

"Hey, guys!" She waved as she walked across the yard.

"Mom, Ruby's giving us a ride!" Tommy shouted.

Logan tugged on Ruby's reins and the horse stopped walking. He smiled when Sadie reached his side. "How's your day going?" he asked.

"Good. Can I speak to you before you take off for Mesquite?"

"Sure." He turned around. "Hey, Gramps, come over here and walk Ruby while Sadie and I talk." Logan took her hand and they strolled around to the front yard.

They stopped by the porch and he studied her face, trying to gauge her mood. The doctor had said he had to train himself to not assume people only wanted to speak to him when he'd screwed up. But this time he couldn't shake the feeling that Sadie was about to tell him something he didn't want to hear."

"I'm flying to Wisconsin for a job interview."

His heart skidded to a stop, then resumed pounding harder than a jackhammer. *What about us?* "I thought you'd planned to keep working at the ranch."

"Tommy was accepted into the special preschool for kids with ADD."

And she hadn't told him?

"This job comes with a big pay raise, which would cover the cost of Tommy's tuition."

"What about trying behavioral therapy like I'm doing?"

"I haven't ruled it out. If Tommy hates the preschool and he and Tyler are miserable being separated, then the extra money in my paycheck will help cover whatever costs my insurance doesn't pick up."

Logan swallowed a curse. He wanted what was best for Tommy, too, but why did it have to be in Wisconsin and not in Stampede?

Desperate to show that everything he did was for her and the boys because he believed they were meant to be a family, he said, "Follow me." He took her hand and they walked to the side yard.

"When did you do this?" She moved closer to the newly plowed vegetable garden.

"Last night after you left with the boys. I wanted to surprise you."

"It's huge." Sadie walked around to the opposite side and examined the rectangle. "What about fencing?"

"Tell me what kind you want and I'll install it."

"A white picket fence would look nice."

He kept talking because he didn't want to think about waking up each day and not seeing her and the boys. "That will work if we attach wire mesh along the bottom to keep animals out."

Sadie strolled around the entire plot, then returned to his side and hugged him. He wrapped his arms around her and held her close, even though he could feel her slipping away. He brushed his mouth against hers, his pulse kicking into overdrive when she pressed herself harder against him. When the kiss ended, he searched for the words to beg her not to go through with the job interview, but a horn honked, catching their attention. He glanced across the front yard and spotted Gunner's truck barreling up the drive. His brother kept blasting the horn. Had something happened to Amelia or Logan's sister-in-law? He and

Sadie hurried to the front yard, where Gramps and the twins met them. Gunner slammed on the brakes.

"What in tarnation is going on?" Gramps grumbled.

Gunner jumped out of the truck, grinning like a clown. He raced around the hood to the passenger side and helped Lydia out of the front seat. She was smiling, too.

The couple walked over to the family and Gunner slipped his arm around Lydia's waist.

"What happened?" Sadie asked.

Lydia held up a scrap of paper. "We're having a girl!"

Sadie squealed and hugged Lydia. "Let me see." Sadie stared at the ultrasound photo.

"See what?" Gramps peeked over Sadie's shoulder.

Lydia pointed to the photo. "It's a picture of our baby."

Gramps grimaced. "Doesn't look like any baby I've ever seen."

"You were right, Sadie," Lydia said. "The nurse in Madison miscalculated and our new due date is March first."

"What do you think, old man, you're going to be a great-grandfather." Gunner slapped Gramps on the back.

"A great-granddaughter sounds nice."

"Can we see, Uncle Gunner?" Tommy asked.

Gunner showed the boys the photo. "That's your cousin."

"She doesn't look like a cousin," Tyler said.

Lydia laughed. "She will when you see her."

"I'm so happy for you." Sadie hugged Lydia a second time, then she ruffled the twins' hair. "You'll love having a girl cousin."

"We don't want a girl cousin. We want a boy cousin." Tommy looked at Tyler. "Right?"

Tyler turned to his aunt. "Can a girl play in a tree house and ride a pony?"

"A girl can do anything a boy can," Lydia said.

Tyler faced his mother. "I guess it's okay if we have a girl cousin."

Everyone laughed, but Logan's chest was too frozen to move. Gunner slapped his back, sending air into his lungs, and he was finally able to breathe again.

"I think my big brother is going to have to build a separate tree house for girls."

"Congratulations." He forced the word from his mouth. Fortunately Gunner was too excited to notice Logan's lack of enthusiasm, but Sadie's stare burned through him.

"I better get going," Logan said. He gave Lydia a quick hug, then walked off to his pickup and drove away. It wasn't until he reached the end of the driveway that he glanced in the rearview mirror.

The sight of Sadie standing alone in the yard staring after his truck sent a sharp pain slicing through his heart. No matter how many hours of therapy he received, or how hard he tried to prove his love to her and the boys, it wasn't enough to keep Sadie from leaving him just like his mother had all those years ago.

Chapter Fourteen

Sadie sat on her aunt's front porch watching the sun come up on the horizon. Nature's beauty calmed the soul—that was one of the reasons she loved gardening. Beautiful flowers made her forget about the struggles and challenges of everyday life.

"You're up early." Aunt Amelia stepped outside and handed Sadie a cup of hot tea.

"Thank you." She set the mug on the table next to her chair.

"I can't believe how fast time is flying by. It seems like you and the boys arrived in Stampede only a few weeks ago, but the end of October is already looming."

"You wouldn't know by the temperature," Sadie said.

"Emmett reads the *Farmer's Almanac* every year and he said we won't get our first freeze until mid-December."

"You and Emmett are getting along better," Sadie said.

"Sometimes women have to knock men over the head to get their attention."

Sadie sipped her tea. She hadn't gotten a wink of sleep last night thinking about the job interview,

Tommy's new preschool and her relationship with Logan. Sadie had planned to continue their discussion about her flying to Madison for the job interview when Logan returned from his therapy session in Mesquite, but he'd made an excuse about needing to check on the construction of the corral near the riding trail, and then he'd skipped supper with her and the boys. Later when it came time for her and the twins to leave the ranch, he was still absent.

Logan had gone to great lengths to prove to her that his ADD wouldn't adversely affect their relationship or his ability to be a good husband and father, but Tommy's future was more important than what Sadie wanted.

"Aunt Amelia, may I ask you a very personal question?"

"No, Emmett and I never slept together in high school. He was always a gentleman when we dated."

"Not *that* personal." Sadie laughed.

"What's on your mind, dear?"

"Why didn't you and Uncle Robert adopt?"

"We should have, but I used the excuse of not wanting the responsibility of raising a child all by myself. Your uncle traveled with his job and was out of town for weeks at a time. But that wasn't the real reason." Amelia blinked hard. "I feared that staring into the face of a child that wasn't mine every day would remind me of my own failure to conceive. I was worried that I'd resent the child and be a bad mother." She sighed. "I should have had more faith in myself."

"So you regret not adopting?"

"I wish my mother or Sara would have challenged my thinking, but everyone pitied me and thought by

not discussing the subject they were doing me a favor."
Amelia patted Sadie's hand. "Fortunately my sisters
allowed me to be a part of their daughters' lives and
I've enjoyed every moment I've spent with you girls."

Sadie searched her heart, thinking she'd always
wanted another child. Logan's acceptance of the twins
had shown her over and over, day after day, that it was
possible to love a child you hadn't conceived. Unlike
her aunt, Sadie didn't doubt her ability to love a child
she didn't give birth to, if that was in her future. "It's
funny how the life we dream of as little girls rarely
becomes a reality."

"That's because we read too many fairy tales and
not enough adventure books."

"You're right. Our childhood was filled with spar-
kly castles and white knights." In real life, castles
became apartments and the white knight cheated on
the princess.

"Are you sure you want to go through with this job
interview?" her aunt asked.

Sadie nodded. This morning when she'd rolled out
of bed she'd almost canceled her flight to Madison
later this evening. "As much as I love Stampede, Aunt
Amelia, I have to do what's best for the twins."

"You mean Tommy," her aunt said.

"What?"

"The special school is best for Tommy but not nec-
essarily for Tyler."

Sadie looked away, unable to refute her aunt's state-
ment. Her shy, quiet little boy had come out of his shell
during their stay in Stampede and now she was going
to rip him away from what made him happy because

his brother needed a special school. Sadie couldn't win for losing.

"I appreciate you and Lydia watching the twins for me while I'm gone."

"Of course. I welcome any excuse to spend more time at the ranch with Emmett."

"I booked an airport limo to drive me into San Antonio later this afternoon. My flight doesn't leave until nine tonight."

"Will you be back in time for Halloween?"

"I should be." Unless she decided to look for an apartment for her and the boys while she was in Madison. "Speaking of Halloween…does Stampede do anything special for the kids?"

"Just the normal trick-or-treating. The weather is usually nice enough to sit on the porch and hand out candy."

"How many kids come by?"

"More than you'd assume. Families who live in the outlying areas drive their kids into town and let them go door-to-door on our block."

"I took the boys to the local rec center to trick-or-treat last year. This will be the first time they've gone door-to-door."

"Lydia and I will take the boys to the Walmart in Mesquite and let them pick out their costumes."

"They'd love that. Thank you." Sadie reached across the table and clasped her aunt's hand. "Have I told you lately that you're my favorite aunt?"

Amelia laughed. "I'm the only one alive, of course I'm your favorite aunt."

"You got a few minutes?" Logan asked when he stepped inside the Moonlight Motel office.

His brother, who stood behind the desk working on his laptop, looked up and frowned. "What happened now? Did the construction crew screw up the stables?"

No one had screwed up anything except maybe him. Sadie had left town yesterday to fly to Madison for the job interview and Logan had been in a state of panic ever since.

"The stables are coming along fine. You should drive out and see them. There's running water, electricity and a working restroom."

Gunner faced the laptop toward Logan. "I've been working on a flyer to advertise the trail ride."

"That looks really good." Logan peered closer at the screen. "I didn't know you could do that stuff on a computer."

"Neither did I. I bought the software on a whim and discovered that I have a knack for this PR stuff."

"Thanks for thinking of the ranch."

"I can design some business cards for the tourist attraction once you and Gramps figure out what you're going to call it."

"Do you have any suggestions for names?" Logan asked.

"I'd stick with something simple like Paradise Trails and Petting Zoo."

"Sounds good to me."

"I've also been tinkering with a new website for the ranch."

"You keep working this hard and you'll ruin your reputation as good-time Gunner," Logan said.

"Ha ha."

"If the website is anything like what you created for the motel, it'll be impressive."

"Me, you and Sadie should sit down and discuss details like hours of operation and prices." Gunner walked over to the coffeemaker and poured himself a cup. "And the ranch will need a Facebook page. People love animal photos. I thought we could teach Gramps how to use an iPhone and have him snap pictures of the zoo animals. I'll post them to the Facebook page."

"That's nice of you to offer."

"I want the ranch and the motel to succeed." He smiled. "When I saw our baby girl in the ultrasound image, I decided right then and there I wasn't going to be like Dad—coming and going in our lives as if we were afterthoughts."

"So no more rodeo for you? Not even for fun?" Logan hadn't expected his brother to adjust to domestic life as well as he had.

"My rodeo career is over—not that I ever had much of one to begin with. But if Ms. Amelia has her way, you and I might have a chance to compete again for fun."

"What are you talking about?"

"Amelia told Gramps the other day that she'd like to bring back the Stampede Rodeo and Watermelon Crawl Festival next May."

"What did Gramps say?"

"He said he'd think about it."

"No way. Really?"

Gunner nodded. "If we can get people to drive to Stampede for the festival, they'll stay at the motel and schedule a trail ride or take their kids to the petting zoo. It's a win-win for everyone."

Logan heard tires squealing and glanced out the window. His grandfather's old jalopy turned into the parking lot and hot on his tail was Amelia in her Thunderbird.

"I have to make a business call." Gunner escaped to the back room, and Logan stepped outside to referee the latest dispute between the old people.

As soon as his grandfather got out of his truck, he pointed his finger in Amelia's direction and said, "She's off her rocker."

Logan's gaze swung between his grandfather and Amelia. Gramps didn't look angry; he looked scared to death. "What's going on?" he asked.

"She's lying like a no-legged dog." Gramps inched closer as if he feared the eighty-five-year-old woman was going to take a swing at him.

"I'm telling the truth, Emmett Shamus Hardell." Amelia planted her fists on her hips and stared at Logan. "I told your grandfather what Sara said to me on her deathbed, but he insists I'm making it up."

Gramps snorted. "How come you kept it a secret all these years?"

Amelia's eyes rounded. "I could ask you the same thing. You're just as good at keeping secrets as I am."

Gramps's face looked as if he'd stood in the sun all day without his hat on. "What secret am I keeping from you?"

Amelia walked closer and pointed to her face. "Look me in the eye and tell me that you haven't had feelings for me all these years."

Feelings? That was what this was argument was about? His grandfather opened his mouth, then snapped it shut. He repeated the action three times before he dropped his gaze and muttered, "You're talking non-sense."

"If I'm talking nonsense, then that means Sara was talking nonsense and she's the most sincere, candid person I've ever known." Amelia wagged her finger. "Sara gave us her blessing to be together because she knew you and I lost our chance because of my stupid mistake."

His grandfather stared, dumbfounded.

"I may not have told you about my conversation with Sara until today, but that doesn't mean it didn't happen."

Logan had heard too much to remain quiet. "What did my grandmother tell you, Amelia?"

"She said she knew Emmett had feelings for me but that he was too honorable to admit to them." Amelia's gaze softened when she looked at Emmett. "Sara was aware that you loved me when you two married, but she knew you'd be faithful."

Logan thought back to the years his grandmother had been alive. She and Gramps had gotten along well—maybe too well. They'd never argued like Gramps did with Amelia. As a matter of fact, his grandparents had acted like best friends, not lovers.

"Maybe I am nutty, Emmett. You're stubborn, rude, grumpy and irrational." Amelia spread her arms wide. "I have no idea why I've never been able to get over you all these years."

Logan watched his grandfather's face transform from doubt to happiness, then back to grumpiness. "And all these years you've been showing me you care by running roughshod over me?"

"It's the only way I knew how to make you notice me."

"Notice you!" Gramps moved away from Logan and said, "How can anyone not notice you living in that fancy house, and driving that fancy car, and throwing your fancy money all over the town."

"It's your fault that I have all this money!"

"My fault?" Gramps looked at Logan. "She's touched in the head."

Amelia snorted. "Don't think I didn't find out it was you who tracked Robert down after he left town. And it was you who bullied him into doing right by me."

The old man stared as if he was seeing a ghost. He cleared his throat. "I couldn't let him get away with doing that to you."

"Well, I wish you would have, because the whole time I was married to Robert I was wanting to be married to you."

Gramps scuffed the toe of his shoe against the pavement.

"Do you know why I've lived alone in that fancy house all these years?" She paused, then said, "Because I can't make myself leave you or this town."

His grandfather's eyebrows shot up.

"As for my fancy car... I've kept it because one day I'd hoped you and I could go for a Sunday drive in it." She sucked in a deep breath. "And about my fancy money... I'm glad I have it because it would have broken my heart if you hadn't been able to buy this motel for Sara."

She faced Logan. "Talk some sense into your grandfather before he dies, will you?" Amelia got into her car and drove off.

His grandfather tugged on Logan's sleeve. "Did I hear her right? She's got feelings for me?"

"From where I stood, Ms. Amelia doesn't just have feelings for you, she's in love with you." A slow smile spread across his grandfather's face.

"Is it true, Gramps? You never got over Amelia after you broke up with her in high school?"

His grandfather's smile disappeared. "It's true."

"Do you regret going after Amelia's husband and making him marry her?"

"Every day."

"What are you going to do about her?" His grandfather stared at the empty highway in front of the motel. "Nothing. We're too old and set in our ways."

"I think you're making a mistake."

"Who are you to lecture?"

"What do you mean?"

"You love Sadie and her boys, but you didn't stop her from going to that job interview up north."

Logan cursed beneath his breath. "It's more complicated than you know."

Gramps motioned to his pickup. "You want to take a drive and bend my ear?"

"Talking won't change what's wrong with me."

"You must be referring to you being sterile."

Logan gaped at his grandfather. "Did Sadie tell you?"

"Nope. Figured it out on my own after watching you and Beth go to so many doctor's appointments. When Beth filed for divorce, I figured it was because you couldn't have kids."

"Beth had gotten pregnant in a previous relationship, but she'd miscarried. When we had trouble conceiving, she thought it might be her. That's why we had all the tests done so soon after we got married."

"It wasn't Beth?"

"I injured myself bull riding the year before I met her. I should have gone to the doctor and had myself checked out, but I didn't."

"There's nothing they can do?"

"Nope. Too much scar tissue now."

His grandfather nodded. "Not sure I see the problem with Sadie. She's already got two boys."

"There's more involved than me not being able to get Sadie pregnant."

"What else is there?"

"It's also my ADD."

Logan had tried his best to prove to her she could rely on him to be an equal partner in a relationship. But his efforts hadn't been enough.

Logan's mind raced back in time to the day he'd accidently bumped into his mother and the bacon grease had spilled all over her arms. Later that night after she'd returned from the doctors, he'd sneaked into her room and had sat on the side of the bed. With tears pouring down his cheeks, he'd promised her that he'd stop running in the house. That he'd quit teasing his brothers. That he'd pay attention to where he was going and what he was doing. But his promises hadn't been enough to keep his mother from leaving.

His grandfather cuffed the back of Logan's head with his hand.

"Ouch! What did you do that for?"

"That was for being stupid."

"Stupid about what?"

"Letting fear keep you from being with the woman

you love." Was his grandfather right? Was he hiding behind his ADD and sterility because he was afraid that once he told Sadie how much he loved her, she'd leave him, too, like his mother and Beth had?

His grandfather was telling him to pledge his love to Sadie and her sons. But would a pledge and his love be enough to keep Sadie happy forever?

SADIE ARRIVED IN Stampede on the thirty-first of October just as dusk descended on the town, and groups of kids were already wandering up and down the block dressed in their Halloween costumes. She'd called after her flight had landed in San Antonio and had spoken with Lydia, who'd assured her that the boys would be dressed in their Halloween costumes and ready to trick-or-treat when the airport limo dropped Sadie off at their aunt's home.

"Thank you." Sadie handed the driver a ten-dollar tip after he removed her carry-on bag from the trunk.

"Have a nice evening, ma'am."

Sadie took the suitcase into the house. "I'm back!" No answer. She went to the staircase in the foyer. "Aunt Amelia? Lydia?" When she returned to the kitchen, she saw the note in Lydia's handwriting stuck to the fridge.

Out trick-or-treating. The boys couldn't wait. We're down the block.

Sadie set her purse on the table and went out the front door. Her aunt had left a bowl of candy sitting on the seat of the rocking chair with a sign that said Help Yourself. She left the yard and joined the goblins, princesses and superheroes, searching for the twins. When she reached the end of the block, she glanced across the street and saw a man in a suit of armor with two miniature cowboys as sidekicks.

Logan. Her heart swelled with love as she crossed the street to join them. She waited on the sidewalk while he escorted the boys to the front door of a house. After getting their treats, the twins turned around. They saw her and raced over.

"Mom, we're cowboys!" Tommy said.

Sadie knelt down for a proper hug, then kissed their cheeks. "I missed you guys."

Tyler straightened his hat. "Do you like our costumes?"

"I love your outfits. You look like real cowboys."

"Uncle Logan says we are real cowboys," Tommy said.

A clinking sound drew closer and Sadie glanced up.

"Uncle Logan's a knight in shining armor," Tyler said.

Sadie straightened. "I see that."

Logan stopped behind the boys and lifted the mask over his face.

He wasn't smiling. In fact, he looked worried. "How was your flight?" he asked.

"Fine." She saw her cousin approaching. "There's Aunt Lydia. Go ask her to walk you to the next few houses. Uncle Logan and I will catch up."

The boys took off, leaving the adults alone. Logan's brown eyes swirled with questions. "How did the interview go?" he asked.

She'd been gone only a few days, but the time away from Logan and the boys had dragged by. "They offered me the job." He opened his mouth to speak, but she cut him off. "And I visited the Busy Little Minds preschool, but as great as the program seemed it was still missing something essential."

Logan's brow wrinkled. "What's that?"

"You."

"Don't leave, Sadie." He sucked in a deep breath, and his chest plate rattled. "Don't take the job. Don't put Tommy in that preschool."

Before she could assure him that she had no intention of doing that, he rushed on. "We've never said the words to each other and it might be too soon for you, but I need you to know that I'm in love with you." He took her by the elbow and escorted her away from a group of kids closing in on them. "I'm not good at expressing my emotions."

"You don't need pretty words to make me fall in love with you." Sadie squeezed his fingers. "Every day you show me why you're the man I want to spend the rest of my life with. The man I want to help raise my sons." She smiled through her tears. "I fell in love with you when you rescued Ruby. I fall in love with you every time I witness your patience with Tommy and your determination to make sure Tyler is never overlooked. I love you a little more each time you demonstrate your devotion to your grandfather. You showed me that I was important to you when you sought help to manage your ADD. You've told me in so many different ways that you care."

He searched her eyes. "I can't give you a baby."

"Another child will not make me happier or more in love with you than I am right now."

"My ADD is never going away. As much as I promise to work hard to keep it in check, there will be times that I totally screw up."

"I'm under no illusion that our life will be perfect. I don't want perfect. I want you. I understand there will be days I'll have to pick up the slack."

"You make it sound simple, Sadie."

"If anyone knows it's not simple, it's me." She caressed his cheek. "But what I feel in my heart when I look into your eyes is stronger, deeper and richer than anything I've felt for anyone in my life."

"There's no special preschool for Tommy near Stampede."

"Tommy will be the luckiest boy in the world to have a dad who understands his challenges. As he grows older, he'll have you as a role model to turn to for advice. No special preschool can offer Tommy the love and guidance you can. And Tyler will flourish because he'll never have to worry he's an afterthought or get pushed aside because of his brother."

"I love you more than you'll ever know." Logan pulled her against him. "I'm the luckiest man in the world."

They smiled at each other, then both of them spoke at the same time.

"Will you marry me?"

"Yes," they answered in unison, then laughed.

Logan's expression sobered.

"I love you, Sadie, because—" he whispered near her ear "—you make my heart go still every time I see you."

"And you said you weren't good with words." She wrapped her arms around his neck. "You know the family will want a wedding, since Lydia and Gunner skipped town."

"I don't care where, when or how we get married—all that matters is that you and the boys and I are a family."

"I like that. A family of our own."

"I love you," he said.

"And we love you." For the first time in her life, Sadie knew for certain that she and her sons were right where they belonged—in Stampede, Texas, with Logan.

* * * * *

If you enjoyed this story, pick up
THE COWBOY'S ACCIDENTAL BABY
to read how Lydia and Gunner
found their happy ending.
And come back to Stampede, Texas,
with the next book in Marin Thomas's
miniseries in 2018!

Western Romance

Cole McCullough must find the birth mother of the twin babies left outside his door. When his ex-girlfriend Stacy Rowe offers to help, he's in for much more than he bargained for!

Read on for a sneak preview of the next heartwarming installment of the **FOREVER, TEXAS** *series,* *TWINS ON THE DOORSTEP,* *by* USA TODAY *bestselling author Marie Ferrarella!*

"You really found these babies on your doorstep?" Stacy asked several minutes later.

She had gotten into the back seat of his truck and he had handed her the wicker basket with the babies. The infants were dozing and the silence in the truck felt overwhelming. Stacy couldn't think of anything else to say, and every other topic would set them off on a course she had no desire to travel.

"Yes, I did," he answered, getting into the driver's seat. He glanced at her over his shoulder.

As if she didn't know where he'd found the babies, he thought.

He was staring at her, Stacy realized, and it took everything she had not to squirm in her seat. This was a totally bad idea, going with Cole to the clinic like this. But no one said no to Miss Joan, and Stacy wasn't about to be the first. She had no desire to have her head handed to her.

"Do you have any idea who the mother might be?" Stacy asked him.

Okay, Cole thought, he'd play along. "There might be a few possibilities," he responded vaguely. "But that's why I came with them to Miss Joan. She's always on top of everything and I figure that she'd be the first to know whose babies they were."

"Miss Joan doesn't know everything," Stacy insisted.

"Maybe," he agreed. "But right now, I figured she was my best shot."

Why are we playing these games, Stacy? Tell me the truth. Are these babies mine?

For one moment, he wrestled with an overwhelming desire to ask the woman in the back seat just that. It would explain why she'd left town so abruptly. But he knew asking her was pointless. He knew her. She wouldn't answer him. In all likelihood, she'd just walk out on him the way she had the last time.

And, angry as he was about her leaving him, he didn't want that happening again. Not until he'd had a chance to talk with her—*really* talk.

*Don't miss TWINS ON THE DOORSTEP
by Marie Ferrarella, available October 2017
wherever Harlequin® Western Romance books
and ebooks are sold.*

www.Harlequin.com

Looking for more satisfying love stories
with community and family at their core?

Check out **Harlequin® Special Edition**
and **Harlequin® Western Romance** books!

New books available every month!

CONNECT WITH US AT:

Harlequin.com/Community

 Facebook.com/HarlequinBooks

Twitter.com/HarlequinBooks

Instagram.com/HarlequinBooks

Pinterest.com/HarlequinBooks

ReaderService.com

**ROMANCE WHEN
YOU NEED IT**

HFGENRE2017R